THE
STRONGER
BROTHER

G.A. SCIBETTA

The Stronger Brother

Copyright © 2023 G.A. Scibetta

Registration number 1201363
Canadian Intellectual Property Office
Category: Literary/Dramatic

Cover Artists
Giustino Scibetta
Angelika Promny-Tavares
Alexandra Asada

Editor
Maryssa Gordon

Library and Archives Canada Cataloguing in Publication

Scibetta-Lawson, Giustino
The Stronger Brother
Published: 2023
ISBN: 978-1-7389975-3-4 (hardback)
ISBN: 978-1-7389975-0-3 (paperback)
ISBN: 978-1-7389975-1-0 (ebook)
1.Title
Further data is available upon request.

00 03 07 28

To my lovely friends.

MUCHAS GRACIAS

Alexandra Asada
Emma Campbell
Sabrina Colella
Chris Couto
Maryssa Gordon
Andrew Lawson
Shaylen Lawson
Sierra Lawson
Megan MacDonald
Angelika Promny-Tavares
Lisa Yannucci

"There is nothing noble in being superior to your fellow man; true nobility is being superior to your former self."

-Ernest Hemingway

do give and GRANT unto _Sir Jacob H. Perkins_ and _his_ heirs, a certain tract or parcel of land

This novel contains sensitive material more suitable for mature readers.

THE
STRONGER
BROTHER

CHAPTER ONE

I always hated this town. Every square kilometre of this place was dreadful. Milton, Ontario, was always my home. I have never lived anywhere but. My family has been situated in the area since the War of 1812, something common for wealthy people like us.

My fifth great-grandfather, Sir Jacob Henry Perkins II, fought for the British side and received the land due to his devoted loyalty to the crown as well as the fact that he knew the acting Lieutenant Governor of Upper Canada personally. Family legend had it that Jacob Perkins had personal blackmail material on the acting Lieutenant Governor, a fellow noble who took over after Sir Isaac Brock died. Unsurprisingly, his threat secured a grant that was overly generous in terms of land size and location. The Perkins dynasty was built upon generational corruption, starting with the first generation. I inherited his name, my full name being Theodore Jacob Henry Perkins I, the first Theodore in the traceable generations.

Over the years, generations of Perkins men built their own estates, each one larger than the previous generation. Our mansion was the largest one ever built on the property. My father built a Mediterranean-revival-style mansion, something that looked like it belonged to a 1960s movie star in old Hollywood. The clay-tiled roof, paired with beige stucco exterior walls, surrounded an interior of lavish high ceilings. The home looked out of place amongst the red-bricked mansions and white-boarded farmhouses that littered the landscape of rural Milton. I was expected to build one even more grand and luxurious one day in place of my father's. This was the epitome of how wasteful and self-conceited my family was. The Perkins family could waste millions of dollars on mansions that were torn down within fifty to sixty years. The whole concept was quite disgusting in my eyes.

My brother, Alexander Henry Andrew Perkins I, or as I called him, Alè, had even stronger opinions than I did in regard to our family. He detested everything about the Perkins family name. In the ninth grade, he even considered legally changing his last name to Dubois to rid himself of the Perkins family curse.

The Dubois family was that of my mother's, a typical French family. My mother wasn't Québécois. She was born Sophie Dubois in a petit village called Sainte-Agnès in the south of France. My mother's French family had nothing. In my father's eyes, they were "peasants." When Alè tried using my mother's maiden name, my father would only refer to him as "my peasant boy" until he eventually became sick of the title. Alè was essentially bullied back into the Perkins family name as my father's tactics worked. On top of that, nobody ever used his preferred last name of Dubois, so he abandoned that notion after about six months.

My father, born with the ridiculous name of Archibald Thomas Alexander Perkins IV, was a brutal man. He frequently picked on Alè and made his life hell.

Because of my brother's attempt to dissociate from our family, I was essentially crowned heir of the Perkins family fortune. My brother was too "unstable" to receive a single penny, according to my father.

"Theo, why didn't you lock the rifle cage, you idiot!" my brother screamed as he threw his skinny body into my door.

"The fuck are you talking about? Alè, you were the one who went up north last. Last weekend you and Tom drove up to—" I began to explain as I was abruptly interrupted.

"Theo, you're full of shit!"

I stared my brother up and down and stopped engaging. I wanted him to match my energy and bring the volume of the conversation back down to earth. He would always get worked up, and this was how I brought his level of intensity to a manageable level.

"Alè, I don't touch the rifles anymore. I haven't in five years," I calmly explained. "I had nothing to do with the rifle cage."

My brother started taking deep breaths, one of the exercises his therapist taught him how to do when he became worked up. I didn't understand why they even brought the rifles last weekend, as it wasn't hunting season. I assumed Tom wanted them in case a rogue bear saw them as fresh meat.

"Uh, maybe it was Arch. Do you think maybe he did it?" Alè asked with an embarrassed tone.

"Maybe, but you can't just barge in here unannounced. What if I was getting changed?"

"Relax, I've seen your micro dick many times."

Alè slowly backed out of my room with a sharp look of embarrassment on his slender face. I could tell he realized I had nothing to do with the hunting rifles after five seconds, but he was too angry to stop himself from lashing out at me. It was possible my father forgot to lock the cage, but it was most likely my brother. Alè's fuse was shorter than most people I had ever come across in my life. A simple bad glance or annoying word could send him into a full-blown spiral. Most people in Milton were scared of him because of that, but I wasn't. I knew my brother had issues, but I never wanted to make him feel subpar because he did. Alè was just different.

I began to make my way down the stairs to the dining room as Maria announced dinner was ready. The whole house smelled of roasted garlic with the slight sour aroma of red wine being decanted in the dining room. Alè didn't bother rushing down, which made my father's anger grow exponentially with every passing second.

"Maria, go get him! The boy is beyond entitled to think we should wait for his majesty's earliest convenience!" my father proclaimed.

Maria quickly shuffled out of the formal dining room and into the front foyer. She then went up the main staircase to the second storey towards Alè's room.

"Theodore, would you be so kind as to pass me the salt?" my father requested while looking up at me.

"You know I prefer Theo. Theodore is too posh sounding."

"I signed your birth registration; therefore, I hold the right to call you by your full name!"

As I gently slid him the salt, my brother's feet clicked across the dark hardwood floors at the entrance of the dining room.

"At last, his majesty King Alexander The Spoiled hath arrived!" my father announced as he mocked a royal bow.

"Arch, must you? Let's just enjoy this nice family meal together," my mother pleaded.

Alè didn't acknowledge my father's comical jab. He just smiled slightly while batting his eyelashes in annoyance. It was the type of smile you give someone when you pass them walking in the neighbourhood, and you barely know one another.

"Maria, this roasted chicken tastes like sawdust! Have Sawyer cook something else! I can't eat this dreadful dish!" my father shouted in disgust.

Maria nodded and quickly ran off with my father's plate. I didn't mind the chicken. Maybe a little dry but fairly edible. Sawyer had always made decent dishes, and this chicken was no exception. I always felt bad for Sawyer when my father sent his dishes back. He always spent an ample amount of time planning and preparing our meals, but my father was almost never satisfied. If I were Sawyer, the thought of poisoning my father might slip my mind from time to time. I know that was horrible, but my father treated Sawyer, Maria, and David like absolute shit. Sawyer was our chef, Maria our housekeeper/butler, and David maintained the exterior of the property. At least David got to work outside, away from my father's commands.

"I read the most interesting article online this afternoon, boys. It stated that boys that grow up without a father figure are more likely to fall into a life of crime and drugs and end up on the streets. Aren't you glad you have all of this?" my father asked as he motioned his arms to the grand dining room surrounding us.

The room was filled with European antiques from my father's personal collection. He had oil frescoes lining the ceilings with a massive crystal chandelier hoisted over the large dark wood table. I found it all quite tacky, but he loved to show this room off.

"So, Simon Carswell, whom I went to elementary school with, is going to be a junkie eventually? You know, since his father is dead," my brother asked as he stared directly into my father's soul.

"Here you go again, twisting my words, as per usual!"

"Well, answer the question!" Alè said.

The dining room became silent while my father put down his wine glass. It was so silent the crystal base made a clink that carried through the entire room.

"Simon Carswell comes from a decent family. His father sadly passed away from a boating accident on Lake Ontario when Simon was young. He has many father-figures in his life that have shaped him into an excellent young gentleman. Simon is not a junk—"

"By decent, you mean rich, right?"

My father shook his head and refused to engage with Alè. I looked over to my mother, who gave me a half-smirk as the tension in the room grew.

"Mr Perkins, I spoke with Chef Sawyer, he can prepare grilled salmon or a beautiful beef tenderloin, but it will be about thirty to forty minutes, sir," Maria explained with a fearful grin.

I could tell she was terrified of having to tell my father that he wouldn't be eating for thirty to forty minutes.

"Tell Sawyer I'm leaving anyway and not to bother."

"Leaving? Where? We haven't sat for dinner for more than ten minutes, and it's Sunday night, Arch!" my mother pressed as she looked at my father with an aggressive stare.

"I'm going out," my father announced with a short demeanour.

"Where are you going?" Alè chimed in.

"Yeah, where?" I added.

"Where! Where! Where! Where!" my brother and I chanted while lightly tapping the table.

"Enough! If I want to see some of my friends, I FUCKING WILL!" my father screamed while banging his massive fists on the table as the bone china clinked.

Alè got his short fuse from our father. It was a Perkins thing. My father scoffed and quickly escorted himself from the dining room as I sat there shovelling mashed potatoes in my mouth. My mother followed behind him like a lost puppy following a stranger in the night.

"What a fucking psycho," Alè whispered.

"Agreed."

We sat there and finished our meal in complete silence. Our family dinner for four quickly became dinner for two due to my father's short temper. As Maria brought out the chocolate cake slices, I finally broke the silence.

"Where do you think he goes?" I asked my brother, pretending not to know.

"Theo, why do you think Mom is so riled? He's definitely going to see his side piece."

"Mom has one too. Let's be real."

My parents hated each other. They only stayed together because they had to keep up appearances. My father was seeing a younger woman, an Instagram influencer who lived in downtown Toronto. Alè and I both knew he was basically her sugar daddy. He provided her with Gucci bags, Chanel perfumes, and girls' trips to Aruba, all in return for sex. It was honestly disgusting knowing my father lived a double life, all while preaching conservative values of "the nuclear family," as he called it.

We were uninformed as to what her name was, as anything we heard about her was through the grapevine of gossip surrounding my family. The root of the grapevine was Uncle Sammy. In fact, the only reason I knew about the mistress was due to my uncle's big mouth. My Uncle Sammy loved to gossip about our family, the main reason my father despised him. Sammy, or Samuel William Henry Perkins II, unfortunately, passed away three months ago after getting into a brutal motorcycle accident. When he died, the grapevine essentially dried out.

My mother was in love with her pilates instructor, Francesco. Francesco had wavy black hair that was parted on the left side and pale white skin. His green eyes shined like sparkly Columbian emeralds every time he spoke to you. He carried an aura of elegance and sophistication no matter what situation he was in.

One night after a night drive, Alè and I came through the front door to find Francesco, and my mother cuddled on the grey velvet settee in our formal sitting room. They quickly jumped up and pretended to have been sitting on opposite sides of the room while having a pot of tea, but we saw what we saw. I knew Francesco adored my mother. I could hear it in the way he spoke about her. I wish Francesco was my father instead of Archibald Thomas Alexander Perkins IV. Francesco Garibaldi actually loved and cherished my mother, something my father was foreign to. When he said the word 'Sophie' in his Sicilian accent, his eyes widened, and his tone softened. He only came around when my father was away or very late at night when my father was sleeping. It was for his own safety as my father would have hung him from the decrepit maple tree on our wooded property.

"Should I clear the plates, boys?" Maria asked as she shuffled behind my chair.

"Yes, I think this shitshow is over," I replied.

Both Alè and I looked up at each other with smiling faces as we both glared over at Maria. Maria was trying so hard to remain professional, but if you looked hard enough, you could see a slight crack of a smile forming from her small pointy face. Maria had been with our family for about seventeen years. She started working with us when I was only one, she was there my whole life. I can't remember a time in my life without Maria. Her family lived back in Puerto Rico, a place she visited for one week a year, as that was all my father would allow. He never once gave her more than her single week in late August.

When she spoke about her family, you could see how emotional the topic made her. She had a son back in Puerto Rico who was five months older than Alè. She

9

always reminded Alè that he reminded her of her precious Jorge. Both Alè and Jorge stood about five foot eleven, had dark brown chocolate hair that was parted down the middle, and they both loved hunting. Maria told us many stories of Jorge hunting the invasive iguanas that invaded the island. Alè's preferred animal was deer. When in season, he hunted deer with his friends near Muskoka, a community a few hours north of the city. I didn't understand how Maria cared for her family so much. To me, my family meant almost nothing.

I only cared for my brother.

CHAPTER TWO

There was an ice-cold stream that ran directly through the middle of our property. As young boys, Alè and I would spend hours playing in the creek, completely covering ourselves in mud and water from the stream. Alè and his friends used to make toy boats and then race the boats down the stream to the end of our property. They loved to do typical boy things, from wrestling matches, making paper aeroplanes, and shooting each other with plastic BB guns in the forest.

As I grew older, I much preferred staying inside and playing with my friend's Barbies. Chloe, a girl who lived three properties over, was in my class at school. She spent every day after school at my house growing up. My parents always joked about how I would one day take her hand in marriage in some grand ceremony at the Royal York in downtown Toronto. I never saw Chloe as someone that I wanted to marry. She was just a friend. Chloe would bring her Barbies over, and we would take turns dressing them up, putting on little Barbie fashion shows in my basement. Maria would always smile when she witnessed it.

Unfortunately for me, my father didn't find my and Chloe's fashion shows to be quite amusing. He referred to them as "games for girls" and eventually forbade Chloe from ever stepping foot in our house again. He constantly reminded me that she was a bad influence on me and took every cheap jab he could at her character.

Chloe and I still kept up our conversations for a little while at school, but eventually, we moved our separate ways. I never blamed her. I couldn't be friends with someone whose father hated me for simply existing. Chloe was a mere personification of the bigger problem in my father's eyes, my lack of masculinity.

I had decided to go for a walk around our property as I had nothing to do. Alè saw me tie up my sneakers by the back door and decided to follow me like he did as a kid. The property was always so pretty in the summer. Summer was the only time of the year rural Milton displayed a sliver of natural beauty. For most parts of the year, Milton was cold, dark, and depressing.

The knee-high grass swayed in the slight breeze that carried the smell of fresh country air. Many people hated the smell of wildflowers and manure, but to me, it was pure bliss. Alè had run ahead, standing in the creek up to his shins.

"The water is freezing, Alè. How are you standing in it?"

"HA! Too cold for Miss Theodora?" he said.

I hated when he called me that. It was Alè's way of taking a jab at my feminine demeanour. I was always careful when teasing Alè back. I knew Alè couldn't bounce back as fast as I did from teasing, so I had to keep my brotherly banter light. If he crossed a line, I still gave it back to him, but if I joked about his appearance or personality traits, he might dwell on the comment for months, sending him spiralling. I cared about his mental well-being too much to do that to him.

"I still can't believe he just dipped mid-dinner yesterday!"

"Can't believe it? That's textbook Archibald shit. He's so dramatic," Alè replied.

"I wonder what he tells her, the woman he fucks."

"What is there to tell? That whore knows he's married, but do you think she cares? Nah, Theo, it probably excites her to sneak around."

"Yeah, but doesn't that make our father even worse? I mean, like he's the one sneaking around, she's kinda smart, like she's literally collecting that bag, sis!" I chuckled in a scandalous tone.

"HA! Collecting that bag, sis? Theo, you have something you wanna tell me?"

I looked at my brother as my face went bright red. I immediately shut down like I always did when people joked about my sexuality.

"She's smart but fuck both of them. I hope they get what they deserve!" Alè blurted out to break the thirty seconds of silence.

"Alè I—" I began to mumble as he interrupted me.

"I was just fucking with you!"

"Alè I uh I uh—"

"T-t-today bro!"

"Alè I actually am—I'm gay," I mumbled under my breath.

"Oh shit! Like deadass for real?" Alè chuckled as he leaned over to hug me.

"Only Jade, and now you know!"

I began crying as I collapsed to the ground. Alè jumped down to comfort me, realizing how difficult the conversation was for me. Alè always tried to laugh his way through difficult conversations. We laid in the long grass as I sobbed like a small child having a tantrum.

"I'm so scared," I cried.

Alè said nothing. He laid beside me, almost completely still, just looking up at the clouds.

"This changes nothing, absolutely nothing," Alè said, breaking his silence.

I reached over to hold my brother's hand. I hadn't held his hand since I was a small child, but it just felt right in the moment. It was so strange being so vulnerable with him, but it was so relieving at the same time.

We laid down for ten minutes, watching the clouds drift by.

"What will our father think of me?"

"Fuck Arch. Fuck Sophie. Fuck anyone who has something to say."

Alè was always the blunt brother, especially behind our parents' backs. If he thought something, he said it, a trait that got him into a few tough situations in his life. People like my father detested his strong spirit, practically seeing it as a threat. My father and Alè clashed like ammonia and bleach. The combination of the two was toxic.

As we laid down in the long grass, a cardinal swooped over our heads. Our property was practically infested with cardinals. In the summer, they nested in a half-dead, decrepit maple tree on our property. In the winter, they hung around the bird feeder on the patio. Their red feathers popped in comparison to the stark white snow. Cardinals always caught my attention.

"See that? When I die, I wanna come back as a cardinal," Alè blurted.

"Die? Dude, you have seventy years to worry about death."

Alè rolled over, facing away from me.

"Yeah," he mumbled.

"Not unless you piss off Arch or something."

"HA! He'd have to shoot me. His fat ass would never catch me!" Alè said.

"Who the fuck wants to come back as a cardinal? At least choose something cool like an eagle or raven. What the hell does a cardinal do anyways?"

"Dude what? The red cardinals get all the ladies! I always see them with the grey-coloured females."

"Oh, so that's why. As a human, you can't get none, so you gotta be cardinal!"

"HA! Funny, coming from the guy who has never had a girlfriend!" Alè said as a wave of realization flooded his mind. "Oh wait! That makes sense!"

"I would come back as a cassowary," I blurted.

"What the hell is a cassowary?"

"Um, the world's scariest bird."

"Theo, there's nothing scary about you!" Alè laughed. "I see you as like a dove or something."

"A dove?" I repeated. "You tryna fight?"

"I'll knock your fruity ass out with one swing!"

We both began to giggle under our breath as we laid on our backs. Alè knowing I was gay was like a million pounds off of my shoulders. Alè's giggling stopped like he had seen a rogue wave whilst out at sea in a dinghy. All of the playful energy quickly dissolved as his aura became distressed and heavy.

"Let's head back to the house," I said as I looked over to my brother.

His face was red and puffy. I wasn't sure if he had been emotional from me coming out or if he wanted to also tell me something. Alè had a hard time speaking about his deep emotions, unfortunately. It was easy to tell when he was in a joking mood and easy to tell when he was pissed off. There was never an in-between. We slowly walked back to the house, but the energy remained heavy. I hated when the energy felt heavy between us.

I had been sitting in my room with my turntable spinning when Maria's voice interrupted the chorus of *Jolene* by Dolly Parton. I loved listening to my Dolly records. The way my soul felt when the vinyl cracked was indescribable. I loved how melodramatic and fierce her voice was, haunting almost as she pleaded for the beautiful woman named Jolene to not ruin her life.

"Dinner is ready, Theo," Maria announced as she gently knocked on my door.

"I'll be down in a minute."

The song still had a few minutes left, but I wasn't going to stop my favourite song early. If my father had anything to say about it, I wasn't going to engage.

The song concluded, and I slid the record back into its paper jacket. I would have preferred to finish the entire album, but I didn't have that kind of time.

As I walked down the stairs from the second storey, I heard the familiar voice of my father's friend Domenico. Domenico Mandracchia was a slimy character that my father hung around when he was in the area. Domenico was once a made member. Once upon a time, he belonged to a prominent crime family in New York that controlled the drug business across the entire east coast. Due to his impulsive behaviour and unwillingness to obey superiors, he was outcasted from his family. The only reason the superiors let him live was due to his father's elite status. Nepotism spared Domenico's life.

I had my suspicions that my father had been involved with Domenico's slimy business ventures for years. Only recently in the last year had I confirmed it after hearing rumours through the grapevine. The money had to have come from somewhere, and being modern-day nobility doesn't pay the bills, especially not the type of money my father spent. My mother detested Domenico. She called him "Dom the Killer." I don't think she was far off with that title.

Domenico most definitely had killed people in his lifetime. His slicked-back grey hair cascaded over his massive head. He wore three rings, one massive diamond on his pinky, his wedding band, and a signet ring on his index finger that had an engraved maple leaf. The maple leaf signet ring was his way of showing he was the boss in southern Canada. It was essentially his crown jewel. He controlled this land with my father's connections. King Charles III may have been King of Canada, but not in these parts.

The room was filled with his signature musky perfume that had notes of fresh cracked black pepper and wealth. You could practically inhale the scent of dirty money radiating from his pores. He always wore a suit. I never once saw him in casual clothing. A charcoal grey custom British-style suit was practically his uniform, nothing off of the rack.

"Wow bello! You're so grown up!" Domenico proclaimed as he watched me enter the dining room.

"Mr Mandracchia, pleased to see you, sir!" I said with a fabrication of false excitement in my voice.

I don't think Domenico picked up on my displeased tone. His smile never broke as he watched me grab a seat. My father was furious that I had just disrespected our unannounced guest, especially because this guest had the power to make us all disappear with a single phone call.

I looked over to Alè, and as our eyes met, he began to chuckle under his breath. My mother lightly nudged my brother to snap him out of his foolish behaviour.

"So Dom, What brings you to the Toronto area this time of year? I figured you would be overseas as you usually are in the summer," my mother asked with a slight smirk.

"What she means is—" my father interjected as Domenico chimed in.

"Business trip!"

"I can speak for myself, Arch," my mother hissed.

"A real fiery wife you have here, Arch!" Domenico chuckled to my father.

"Indeed!"

The room became silent as you could hear silverware scraping the plates from everyone sitting around the table. I hated sitting in silence, so I needed to spark up something.

"Domenico, how has the weather been in New York? I would love to see the city one day," I announced.

"Hot and humid. Everyone in New York has been complaining that street trash is festering in the heat. I think New Yorkers just love to complain!"

"Wow! I think I'll wait til the fall," I replied with an awkward laugh.

"If you're ever in New York, give Zio Dom a call. I'll show you around."

"Will do."

I was such a convincing liar. Had I been in New York City, Domenico Mandracchia was the last person I was going to call. I knew he would probably try to indoctrinate me into his world of underground crimes. The Perkins family would never be made members of his newly-formed gang, as we lacked Italian ancestry, but we were rich and powerful in Ontario, something that was of value to Domenico and his gang of goons.

"Alexander, how is school? I thought you would have graduated high school at nineteen?" Domenico asked.

"I never graduated, Zio Dom. I have to do my diploma recovery courses online,"

"Bah! Just like your father, eh Arch?" Domenico laughed as he caught my father's displeased glance.

"Oh, is that true?" I smirked.

Alè stared down my father with a quarter-smile, scanning his face.

"I'm doing a victory lap as well. I'm trying to upgrade some courses because I want to apply to a few schools next year," I said.

"Good for you!" Domenico smiled.

My father didn't engage with a single one of us. Domenico knew he had crossed a line, so he backed down from the topic of my father's studies. Domenico and my father studied at NYU together before Domenico dropped out to carry on the family business. My father most likely bribed his secondary school teachers so that his grades were good enough for university if Domenico had told the truth about my father's academic habits.

"Mr Perkins, the main course will be ready in two minutes. Shall I clear the appetizer dishes?" Maria asked with a soft tone.

"Take them away!" he barked. "Don't ask. Just do it."

Maria circled the table with a defeated face, clearing our dishes one by one. I felt bad for her as she had to work alone. Part of me wanted to jump up and help her, but part of me knew my father would throw a fit. He believed all Perkins were "above" that type of work. He constantly enforced that we were above many things, clearing dishes included.

Dinner concluded about forty minutes later while Domenico and my father retired to the front den to sip on some fine French brandy. I found brandy to taste like the smell of gasoline, but my father was quite obsessed. I overheard the men discussing politics, Donald Trump this, Trudeau that. It was all very boring and repetitive. Every few minutes or so, one of the men would crack a joke, and the other would let out a stupid laugh. I detested both of their laughs.

Domenico tied his leather oxfords as he headed for the driveway well after midnight. His stark-white SUV fired up as his LED bulbs lit up our front entryway. He slowly backed out while my father waved him farewell. I quickly sprinted upstairs as soon as I saw Domenico back out.

As I walked past Alè's bedroom on my way to the bathroom, I noticed his door was cracked, and he was writing in his journal.

"Dear Diary, today was totally freaking shit—"

"Shut the fuck up, Theo!"

I smiled at him to let him know I was just playing around. As he closed the journal, I jumped on my brother's bed, almost launching his skinny body off of the edge.

"Did you know Domenico, sorry, *Zio Dom* was coming?" I asked in a sarcastic tone.

"Nobody did. He's like a tumour. He just appears."

"He seriously creeps me the fuck out!"

"Theo, he creeps everyone out. Arch keeps him around for the money opportunities."

"Money or fear?" I shot back.

"Both."

Alè laid his head down on his pillow, sinking into his bed in pure exhaustion.

"Theo, do you remember Skylar?"

"Skylar Petipas, your ex-girlfriend from, like, the eleventh grade?"

"Yeah."

"Um yeah, that's rand—" I replied as I was cut off.

"Do you think I'm too impulsive?" Alè inquired with a sad glare.

"WHAT? Where is this coming from?"

"Answer the question."

"No, you lead with your heart Alè. It's quite admirable. You can sometimes be quick to jump when it comes to decision-making, but your decisions always make sense," I said in a reassuring tone.

"Skylar left me in the eleventh grade, and that was her main reason for dumping me."

"Fuck Skylar with her stupid little ponytail. That hair ain't even cute."

"HA! Leave it to my gay brother to comment on her haircut!" Alè said.

"SHH! Mom is upstairs. She can fucking hear you!" I yelled as I stared my brother down.

Alè just giggled at my demand to lower his voice. His giggling then transformed into a smile, which transformed into a slight frown. Then, suddenly, a few tears rolled down his chiselled cheekbones. He sat up and stared through me.

"Alè, are you okay?"

My brother collapsed as he fell into my arms. I knew something was very off about his energy, he was sitting in front of me on the bed, but he was not present in that bedroom. Rather, his soul was off in the abyss. It was so strange to see my brother so emotional. He never showed me that side of him.

"I love you, bro," he whimpered to me as he sobbed.

"Shit, I'm chokin' up here," I replied as I gently tapped my brother's back.

We sat on his bed for twenty minutes. I stared out of his window at the trees where the cardinals sat all day. Since it was closer to one o'clock in the morning, the trees sat vacant of the red-feathered birds.

"What made you think of Skylar? Why now?"

"Dunno, just thinking."

"Yeah, but Alè, it's been years!"

"I still love her. I still think about her every day," Alè proclaimed.

"Have you tried speaking to her since? Maybe send her a text or—"

"I'm blocked on everything."

"Hmm."

"See that tree? The first time Skylar and I made love, she told me that large maple tree looked like something out of a Tim Burton movie," Alè explained with a slight chuckle.

"Made love? Okay, Romeo, you have shagged bare girls up here."

"I didn't shag Skylar. We made love."

"HA!"

"You, Skylar, Maria, and Sawyer were the only ones I ever cared about in my life."

"Were? I'm not dead!" I said.

"Sorry, ARE the only ones."

We sat in silence as my brother fixated on the sad, decrepit maple tree in the yard. He only broke his stare to blink every few moments.

Skylar Petipas came from a "less-fortunate" family, my father would always say. She was poor. She barely had enough money to wear clothes without holes in them. My father hated Skylar because of this. He made his hatred known. He never once tried to conceal it. As Skylar would join us for dinner on an occasional night, my father would take open jabs at her in front of any other guests that were joining us. Skylar cried almost every time she came over due to something my father had said. He once referred to her as "a byproduct of meth" due to her mother's difficulties with addiction. He made it clear she was an addict's child, an accident of some sort. My father investigated the background of every girlfriend Alè brought home, but Skylar's background interested my father the most. Despite my father's complete lack of human decency for Skylar, my brother still loved her, all of her, good and bad. I knew

Skylar used my brother's 'impulsivity' as an excuse to get away from my father. Archibald drained all of the joy out of my brother's life, every last drop.

I got up from his bed and started pacing around the room. As I walked over to his desk, I noticed Alè still had his original copy of Queen's *A Night at the Opera* sticking out of his milk crate of records.

"Remember when we would fight over this when we were kids?" I asked as I grabbed the record from the crate.

"You ruined every song with your scratchy voice," Alè said with a slight smile.

"Whatever! When you sang along with Freddie, he came back from the dead to ask you to shut the fuck up."

Alè began to laugh hysterically at my stupid joke. I didn't expect such a reaction from him.

"I never play it. Keep it."

"Huh, are you drunk or something?"

"No, seriously, keep it! I never play records anymore. My stylus snapped off about eight months ago, and I can't be bothered to order a new one."

"Dude, it takes one tap on your phone, and one will be here tomorrow," I shared in a confused tone.

"Nah, all yours, brother."

I took the record and walked towards my bedroom. As I walked down the hall, I could see Maria carrying my mother a cup of herbal tea. I hated that my parents made her work in the middle of the night. The poor woman deserved some sleep like the rest of us.

CHAPTER THREE

I awoke to the sound of screaming radiating across every room in our house. My brother's voice was the most prominent sound coming from the kitchen, so I shot out of bed to investigate. As I threw on my grey sweatpants and a T-shirt to cover my naked body, I heard the footsteps of Maria pass by my closed door. I cracked my door open and started making my way down to the kitchen as she had been bringing my mother a cup of her morning coffee in bed. I never made Maria bring me food or drinks to my bedroom. That was something I took pride in doing for myself. Maria was not my servant. She was family in my eyes.

"Right! You know so much at the ripe age of nineteen!" my father screamed at Alè.

"I'm old enough to know when I'm being talked down to!" my brother shouted.

"Talk down? All you do is talk down to me!"

"You deadass start every fucking fight!"

"Dead-ass? Surely you have a more diverse vocabulary to be using words like that! Although, I shouldn't expect anything less from my stupid son!" My father chuckled.

I turned the corner to the kitchen as both my father and brother looked over at me.

"What the hell is all this noise for?" I probed.

Neither my brother nor my father said a word to me. My father scoffed and stormed out of the kitchen towards the front den. Alè looked up at me with a red and puffy face, looking like he was about to burst into tears. I couldn't blame him though, as being called stupid by your own father must've cut deep. Alè walked past me and shuffled up the stairs as if he was carrying fifty pounds of dead weight on his back. I had seen elderly people at the mall climb stairs faster with their busted hips and ailments.

I walked into the kitchen to make myself my morning espresso, as I needed my dose of caffeine before diving into all of the drama. As I started the machine, my father re-entered the kitchen to investigate what I was doing.

"You know, Maria makes the best espresso," my father jeered.

"Yeah, she taught me how."

"Taught you?" my father asked with a puzzled face.

"Yup."

"But that's what she's here fo—"

"I'm eighteen. I'm fully capable of preparing my own coffee!" I interjected.

"Well, since you're so grown up, maybe you can start paying rent around here," my father mocked.

I ignored his jab and kept tamping the grounds in the hopper while the water bled from the line.

"You know, she doesn't have to do everything for us!"

"Why should you or I lift a finger? We are practically royal if you trace our bloodlines, start acting like it!"

"Aye, yes, Milton, what a lovely kingdom we oversee thy father," I mocked as I bowed down.

"That's not even correct old English. Maybe YOU are the stupid son."

"Perhaps Lord Perkins, perhaps!"

My father scoffed as he knew he wasn't able to get under my skin like he could with Alè. I smiled slightly as I watched his fat body waddle out of the kitchen in a slightly defeated stride.

In the past, I had always cowered down to my father, but after I had come to the revelation that Archibald was a bully, I no longer respected him the way I once did. Deep down, I always knew he was a bully. I just chose not to see it as such to keep the peace within Perkins Palace. It was only until I realized how much of an effect my father's bullying had on my brother's mental health that my respect disintegrated. I regretted not acknowledging it sooner.

"I think you're an excellent barista, Theo!" Chef Sawyer mumbled in a low tone so that my father couldn't hear.

"Have you been here this whole time?"

"No, I was just taking inventory of the pantry, and I accidentally overheard you guys," Sawyer explained.

"HA! Half of Milton overheard Lord Perkins and his screaming match with Alè."

Sawyer looked at me and started to slightly grin. I knew he was holding back a full-blown laugh, but he didn't want to risk mocking my father, despite knowing that I would never rat him out.

"What are you making tonight?"

"Lamb, maybe grilled, with sautéed asparagus and a side of garlic mash."

"Shit! I'm gonna be out tonight. That sounds delightful, Chef."

"Oh, no worries. I can set aside a separate portion and cook it later when you arrive."

G.A. Scibetta

"No need. I could be out late. I'm taking the train to see a comedy show at Scotiabank Arena tonight!"

"WOW! Lucky!"

"Right! My girlfriends from school will be there, so it's going to be a wild night!"

"Girlfriends? More than one?" Sawyer asked.

I awkwardly laughed to shut down the conversation that I had walked myself into. Straight guys didn't call their friends "girlfriends."

"What's the comedian's name?" Sawyer asked.

"Tony DiMattina. He has a show on Netflix!"

"My daughter loves him!" Sawyer said with excitement.

"You have a daughter? You never told me about this Chef!"

"Yeah! She's eighteen as well. You and Isabelle would make a great pair."

"Where does she live?" I asked.

"Oh, nowhere near here. She lives in Parry Sound with her mother."

I could see in Sawyer's eyes he was genuinely happy that I took an interest in his personal life. I felt quite embarrassed that I had known him for many years and had just now found out about his daughter, who was my age.

"How does Isabelle feel about you working so far from her?" I inquired.

Sawyer looked at me in shock that I took his feelings into consideration. He was practically too stunned to speak.

"We miss each other."

"I'm—I'm sorry."

28

"Anyways, I have to start doing some prep work. Talk later, Theo."

"Don't work too hard, Chef!"

Sawyer winked at me, then turned around and started walking back to the pantry. Our pantry looked like something out of a restaurant, not something you would see in a home. There were shelves of the freshest ingredients, imported from all over the world. That room was Sawyer's personal haven. I didn't see the appeal. There were no snacks or junk food, just expensive ingredients.

I closed the interior garage door behind me as my mother fired up her silver Mercedes G-Class. Both of my father's women drove a G-Class. My father reportedly bought his mistress one as well last year at the same time. Almost every influencer had a pink-wrapped exterior, at least every influencer I followed, anyways.

We flew down the driveway and had to briefly slow down to allow the electronic front gate to open. I always found it strange that we had a gate as it was practically for display. If someone wanted to get on our property, the decorative iron gate was surely not stopping them.

"So what time am I picking you up from Bronte Station?" my mother asked in an annoyed tone.

"Dunno, maybe midnight."

"That's too late, Theo! You're eighteen!"

"Well, I could've driven myself to the station. I have my G2 permit!"

"I don't care about driving you! I just don't want my son wandering the streets of Toronto at midnight!"

"It's fine. Emily and Jade will be with me the whole time."

"The whole time?"

"Well, they are getting on at Oakville Station," I replied.

"Why?"

"Cuz Emily lives like two minutes from Oakville Station."

"You guys better walk right to the arena from Union. It's a two-minute walk, no wandering, Theo!"

"Yes madam!" I said sarcastically.

"I'm serious, Theo! There's a lot of sketchy people in Toronto!" my mother pleaded.

"Mom, there's a lot of sketchy people in our dining room."

My mother started to slightly chuckle as she knew I was referring to Domenico's visit.

"Do you know where you guys are going to eat?"

"Dunno, maybe something greasy, something easy."

I started playing music from my phone over the speakers, hoping my mother would take the hint that her interrogation should stop. She started bobbing her head to the beat and mumbling some of the words she knew. I didn't mind hanging out with my mother when she wasn't near my father. Sophie was a completely different person when Archibald didn't have his leash on her. I liked seeing that side of her, a more youthful and light-hearted side.

We pulled into the train station parking lot with only two minutes until the train's departure. I quickly thanked my mother for driving me then I started jogging through the tunnel to my platform. The doors nearly closed on me as I boarded the moment they shut behind me. The train was empty, something unusual for a Toronto-bound train.

I looked up as I caught a glimpse of Jade walking by herself down the aisle of the train. To my surprise, Emily was not with her.

"Sooooo," Jade began to dramatically explain.

"Wher—" I began to ask as I was cut short.

"Emily and I had a big fight about an hour ago. She told me she doesn't want to go tonight now!"

"Fight? What? Why?"

"Do you have a minute? This shit is long!"

"Tell me your fucking with me! She's getting on at Clarkson Station or something in five minutes!"

"Nope," Jade uttered under her breath.

I stared directly into Jade's light brown eyes. I wanted to see if she would break her act and tell me that Emily was actually going to the show. I could tell by her glum demeanour she was dead serious.

"What happened, Jade?"

"So, uh, remember how Emily borrowed my foundation once, and I told her the shade was not a match?"

"Yeah."

"Well, we were getting ready for tonight at Emily's house, and she started using my concealer to cover her under-eye circles. I told her again, which set her off!"

"Your concealer? Jade, um—"

"Theo, I'm black! Emily is white!" Jade howled.

The sound echoed across the whole train car as Jade, and I began to laugh uncontrollably. I almost started to tear up as I hadn't laughed this hard in months. It was much needed, given all the Perkins family drama and constant tension I lived through.

"I'm white, and Emily is too pale for my concealer!" I chuckled.

"HA! I love her but damn! She told me that she needed a break from me. I'm gonna give that girl some space to clear her head."

"I love her too, but damn."

The train pulled into Union Station, and we let everyone else get up before making our way to the doors.

"Wait, what do we do with her ticket?" I inquired.

"Soooo—"

"What? Did you sell it to an online scalper?"

"Not exactly," Jade smirked.

"Spit it out, babes!"

"I invited a really cute guy that I met at a party last summer," Jade explained.

"Met a party? So a stranger?"

"No! We have hung out a bunch of times, but I kinda have a small crush, if I'm being honest."

"Great! Theo the third wheel!" I sarcastically proclaimed.

"No, it's not like that. He's great! I promise we will all hang out as friends, Theo! His name is Wesley."

"Sure."

"I'm serious. He's great. My mom loves him!" Jade smiled.

"You brought him home to meet your mom? So things must be serious!" I laughed.

"HA! No! I'm honestly just his friend, Theo!"

"Sure."

As we walked through the station, Jade began to text her friend Wesley. I didn't want to be a buzzkill, so I tried to mentally prepare myself to meet this new friend of hers. We walked into the Great Hall. The Great Hall had some of the most beautiful architecture in the whole city. Some people called it the 'fake Grand Central Station.' I looked across the hall, and there was the most beautiful boy I had ever laid my eyes on, waving at Jade.

"Wesley, this is Theo!" Jade explained.

Wesley hugged Jade, then quickly turned over to hug me! I was shocked as my family had always ingrained in me that hugging was reserved only for close family and some friends. I found the action quite strange, almost unnatural.

"So, Theo, how did you and Jade meet?" Wesley asked as his blue eyes shimmered in the station lighting.

"Oh, Jade and I went to elementary school together. We have always been in the same circle."

"Damn! Am I crashing your date night?" Wesley asked with a chuckle.

"Oh, no, Jade and I are—"

"I was just messing with you, Theo."

"So Wesley, are you excited to see Tony?" Jade chimed in.

"Duh! He's the hottest comedian alive! I have had his poster on my bedroom wall forever!"

I stared at Wesley as he had just referred to a male comedian as hot.

"Oh, I'm bi, by the way," Wesley added.

"That's cool. It's fine by me, like—"

"Theo, he doesn't need your approval!" Jade said.

Wesley and Jade began to chuckle, and I awkwardly joined in.

"I was—No like I—What I meant—Like I want—"

"HA! It's okay, Theo. I know what you meant," Wesley explained with a flirtatious smile.

The three of us awkwardly walked through Union Station and exited towards the street. It was possible to walk into Scotiabank Arena without leaving Union, but both Jade and Wesley wanted to have a smoke before the show. Jade bummed one of Wesley's cigarettes as she wasn't old enough to buy them. Wesley was nineteen, so he could buy them, the legal age in Ontario.

Wesley's wavy blond hair moved in the slight breeze that drifted down Front Street. His body stood about six feet, something I found very intriguing. While they both sucked back their smokes, I caught Wesley staring at me about five times. His sapphire blue eyes sparkled at me, and he was confident enough to not break his stare every time I caught him. I wasn't sure if he could sense I was gay or if he was just so into me that he didn't care what my sexuality was.

We entered at the Bay Street doors after strolling around the block, as Jade had our tickets scanned at the door. Jade walked ahead as Wesley saw the opportunity to walk beside me and strike up a conversation.

"So, how long have you been a fan?" Wesley asked with a flirtatious smirk.

"Oh, I have been a hardcore fan even before his Netflix show!" I announced.

"Mmm, doesn't surprise me." Wes smirked.

"Okay Wes, what's that supposed to mean?" I asked with a grin.

"Wes? You've known me for twenty minutes, and you already gave me a pet name," he said.

My face went bright red as I wasn't sure if I should be openly flirting with him. I had shown interest in and hooked up with guys in secrecy in the past, but flirting in public felt so intimate to me. It was easy to flirt with Wesley. Our personalities seemed to mesh instantly.

"I'm just fuckin' with you, T. You can call me Wes," he said.

"T? Mmm, who's giving out pet names now?"

"Oh shit! They have his newest act recorded on vinyl! We gotta snag one each on the way out!" Jade announced as she turned around to Wes and me.

"Duh!" I yelled.

"I only listen to music on vinyl, not talking," Wes said.

I wasn't sure if she had heard us blatantly flirting or if our voices were muted by the rambunctious halls of people and stadium sounds.

"Does Mr Wes have a record player?" I asked.

"Duh!" he said while mocking me.

"Rude!"

Jade got in line for some popcorn and a soda. I was too nervous in Wesley's presence to eat anything, so I waited off to the side with him. I didn't want him to think of me as a slob, shoving buttery popcorn down my throat.

"Have you ever gone vintage record shopping in the city?" Wes asked.

"Never. I just order all my records online," I replied.

"Oooh, we should go. It would be fun!"

"A date? He moves fast, damn."

Wes grinned while playing with his luscious blond locks.

"Wait, do you live in the city?" Wes asked.

"By the city, you mean Milton?"

"So you're not a Turrono Manz?"

"Turrono Manz?" I asked.

"Yeah, that's what we call ourselves."

"One day, I wanna be a Turrono Manz, but for now, I'm stuck in the mud," I said while rolling my eyes.

Jade overheard me refer to my home as 'the mud.'

"He lives in a royal palace, Wesley. You should see it!" Jade said in a slightly snarky tone.

I knew Jade could feel the chemistry between Wes and me. I didn't intend to make her jealous, as I knew she had a crush on Wes, but flirting with Wes was just so easy. Being partially closeted, I rarely flirted with guys in public. I had come out to Jade about three months ago while sleeping over at her house. She essentially told me she always knew, something I didn't know whether to be content with or offended by. I was still in the process of figuring out who I wanted to know about my sexuality. I was not keen on telling my parents. I actually never wanted to tell them.

"A royal prince? I wanna see this palace where Prince T resides!" Wes said.

"Trust me, you would rather not."

"Mmm, why?" Wes asked.

"Let's just say the king and queen are not so welcoming," I explained.

"I see."

"The king hates me," declared Jade.

"Oh, defo!" I said.

The comedy show started about thirty minutes after we took our seats in the upper bowl, three rows from the top. Jade's mother had bought us the tickets as Jade's Christmas present the previous year. Jade's mother didn't have a ton of money, but she adored her daughter endlessly, a concept I was foreign to.

Tony DiMattina entered the stage with a gorgeous sparkly blazer that caused tiny light ripples across the whole stadium. Even from the top deck, his stage presence asserted its dominance in every attendee's eyes. Every joke he cracked was eccentric, almost as eccentric as his outfit. I forgot all of my problems the more he spoke, even if it was only for a couple of hours. I was in a good place mentally, something very rare for me.

As his last bit finished and the stage lights went out at Scotiabank Arena, a wave of reality rushed over me as I reentered planet Earth. My soul was off into the abyss and had just reconnected with my body back in the jam-packed concert hall in Toronto. I looked over my shoulder to see Jade and Wes both wiping tears from their eyes. They had been laughing so hard that their tears did not come as a shock.

"I think I'm in love!" Wes proclaimed.

"What did I just witness?" Jade yelled out as both Wes, and I leaned in to hug her.

"I wish I had the balls and style to pull off a sparkly blazer!" I announced to the two of them to disturb the moment with humour.

Both Wes and Jade began to lightly chuckle as we slowly broke our hug.

"T, you could pull off anything!" Wes announced with a slight smile.

I slowly turned to look at him directly in the face. I could feel the slight aura of awkwardness radiating from

Jade's body as her love interest had just openly compli-
mented my body while she was sandwiched between us.

"Let's go shopping tomorrow, just the three of us.
Maybe at the Eaton Centre or something!" Jade awkwardly announced to change the subject.

"Yes! Love that idea!" I abruptly expressed.

We made our way out of the arena as the crowd began to disperse, pushing our way past all of the obsessed
fans. Jade was so perplexed that she stormed right past
the vinyl record stand in the concourse that she men-
tioned earlier she wanted to shop at. Both Wes and I kept
glancing back at each other in confusion as she stormed
six feet ahead of us. We eventually reached the entrance
of Union Station while Jade began to dial a number on
her phone.

"Are you guys heading back home now?" Wes asked
in a disgruntled tone.

"Dunno, maybe. Jade is talking to someone, so I'm
not sure what she has planned."

Wes and I looked over to Jade, who had been standing about fifteen feet away while making a phone call.
Her face seemed excited, almost like she was making
plans to throw a party with whoever was on the line.

"So, Prince T, what's your Instagram?"

"Mmm, maybe I don't have Insta, Wes."

"Don't you royals love to post? I think I follow your
cousin King Charles on Insta," Wesley said.

"Ah yes, cousin Charles, we go way back. We meet
for tea every Wednesday at Buckingham Palace. His
team picks me up. It's great!"

Wes chuckled at my joke while he leaned in to embrace me. His body felt like I was hugging a marble stat-

ue carved by Michelangelo. He was more beautiful than any statue I had ever seen on my annual summer trips to Italy or France. As his body fell into mine, his captivating perfume transferred onto my skin. As he ended our embrace, I began radiating his scent.

"Change of plans! I'm going to see Hayley Campbell. She saw on my story that I was in the city, so she invited us to her party!" Jade abruptly explained.

"Oh, uh, I think I'm gonna go home. My parents want me back at a decent time," I explained.

"Sorry, Jade, I have to get back to my apartment. I can't stay out until the sun rises. I know how you party!" Wes elaborated with a slightly awkward chuckle.

"No problem! Well, I'll see you guys tomorrow!"

Wes hugged Jade and then turned over to me to do the same. Our hug was substantially longer than theirs. It was blatantly obvious Wes was into me, undeniable almost. I was too focused on Jade's shady behaviour. I could not believe she had the nerve to spring these last-minute plans on me. She knew Hayley and I hated each other. We had since day one. Hayley even bullied me for a period of three months in the second grade. She referred to me as the 'brat boy' as she hated that I came from money. Hayley picked her next gossip victim and focused on them while I was supposed to pretend the bullying never happened. She acted like those three months were irrelevant now. I was not in the mood to pretend to be anyone's friend, especially not Hayley's.

I boarded the return train from Union. I popped in my earbuds to blast some cheesy love songs, something I felt drawn to. Every song brought the image of Wes to my mind. His scent triggered something in my brain, something I couldn't ignore.

After two stops, my phone lit up with an Instagram notification. I quickly glanced at my lock screen to see @wes.summers35 had sent me a direct message. My heart fell out of my chest and rolled down the train corridor into the tracks below. I found the fact that he searched me up both romantic and slightly forward at the same time. I became quite flustered as I read the paragraph he sent.

Wes: *Hey T! Um idk how to rly say this but ur cute. Do you wanna graba coffee or something tomorrow before we go shopping? I'm sry if this is too forward but I wanna see u!*

Theo: *Wow he rly found me thru Jade's profile what a creeper! Ofc I wanna see u Wes, ur cute too*

Wes: *Wait r u gay? U dont gotta like tell me rn but im just curious*

Theo: *Yea, but like im not out to anyone tho. Like just my bro and Jade know. Well u do too now but like it's on the the down low*

Wes: *No prob! Im not sayin shit Prince T :) Anyways see u tom before shopping. I know the cutest cafe by my place. Night T <3*

Theo: *Can't wait :) Night Wes <3*

I excitedly smiled and gushed the whole train ride home. Wesley's messages made an awkward night exciting once again. I wasn't shocked that he messaged me. He had already tried to ask for my Instagram at Union.

As I left the train, I noticed my mother's car parked across the lot. I looked into the driver's seat, shocked to see Maria had come in my mother's place. Maria hated driving my mother's car, so the sight alone was confusing.

"Hey Maria, wher—"

"Your mother went out," Maria said.

"Oh, but where did she go—"

"Out!" Maria snapped.

Maria was hiding something. I could tell from her eyes that she knew something that I didn't. Her answers were very brief. She clearly didn't want to elaborate or was scared to elaborate rather. We drove for about ten minutes in complete silence.

"She's out with Francesco!" I abruptly proclaimed.

Maria's eyes widened, and she turned her head to her left so as to not disclose her look of shock. I knew I was right, Maria and I were emotionally intertwined, and I knew how her mind worked.

"Maria, I'm not a kid. I know my parents hate each other."

"Deep down in their hearts, there is love."

"Deep down in Archibald Perkins' heart, there is tar. Black and sticky like his soul."

Maria began to bow her head down in defeat. She knew she could no longer lie to me at my age. I was becoming a young adult, an analytical one to boot.

"Theo, your father has been broken by things outside of his control."

I stared at Maria's face in pure shock. This was the first time she had ever spoken out against my father so openly. Her Puerto Rican accent made the declaration almost poetic. I wanted that line on a T-shirt.

"I know," I mumbled.

"I love you, Theo."

Maria's eyes began to slightly water.

"You're one of the only people I love, Maria."

We cruised out of the city lights and back into the countryside. All the joy drained from my body the darker the sky became around us from the fading light pollution. We got closer and closer to hell.

CHAPTER FOUR

I woke up to silence. Silence was a strange occurrence in our home, practically unheard of. There was no fighting, no screaming, and no obnoxious guests of my father's. Well, not complete silence. Our groundskeeper, David, was mowing the front lawn, so I could hear the faint buzz of the mower in the distance. I quickly threw a sweater over top of my body and threw on some of Alè's sweatpants that Maria mixed up while doing our laundry. He was thinner than I was, so they fit like yoga pants. Alè was essentially built like a pencil. I was thin, but nowhere near as thin as my brother. We could barely share any clothing items. I shut my bedroom door behind me and made my way downstairs. Alè was sitting at the dining room table alone. He never ate breakfast at the dining room table, especially not alone. We only used that room with its ornate antiques and tacky interior when we had our family dinners or when my father invited some wise-guy-type character over.

"Morning," Alè yelled as he caught a glimpse of me making my way down. "Nice pants, sexy!"

"What are you doing?" I asked my brother.

"Eating breakfast Theo, as people do," Alè said sarcastically.

"No shit, but why are you in here?"

"Just am."

"Weird," I said as I raised my eyebrows.

I just stood in the doorway and stared my brother up and down, smirking at him to attempt to make him smirk back. Despite my efforts, he never returned a smirk.

"I've got my eyes on you," I said as I held my stare.

Alè's face looked like he was avoiding something. He hadn't eaten breakfast in the formal dining room since he was a small boy. It was like he was trying to relive his early childhood in a way. Even the food he was eating was not something he typically ate. Rye toast with peanut butter and blueberry jam. Alè ate that breakfast every day before elementary school in that exact chair, something he randomly decided to relive this morning. The whole scene didn't sit right with me, but I couldn't quite understand why.

I walked over to the kitchen to fix myself some breakfast and saw Sawyer, struggling to start the espresso machine. Maria typically made the coffee in the house. Sawyer was new to our machine. Maria was nowhere to be seen, something that was also strange for our house. This whole day was strange.

"Imagine being a chef but not knowing how to make an espresso!" I said as Sawyer glanced up at me, smiling.

"Your father is on the back patio. He requested I make him an espresso," Sawyer said with a look of panic.

"Requested or demanded?" I asked with a grin.

Sawyer began to smile then he let out a small giggle. I felt like I had succeeded in making him laugh at my father.

"Where's Maria?" I inquired while Sawyer tried to tamp the coffee grounds.

Sawyer looked at me and motioned for me to come in close. He checked over both shoulders to ensure we were alone.

"She's out looking for your mother. She was picked up by a friend last night. They drove a black sedan," Sawyer whispered with widened eyes.

"Oh, I see."

I knew exactly who she had been picked up by. It was very bold of Francesco to pick her up from our house while my father was home. My parents must've had a really intense fight if he showed up here. It was either that or my father had been asleep.

"So you have to make sure there's enough water in the tank, then bleed the lines before you pull your shot of coffee," I explained, trying to change the subject.

Sawyer was perplexed that I wasn't shocked by his gossip. I knew all about Francesco and his fancy black sedan.

"I always mess this part up!" Sawyer said with a smile.

"Here I'll show you!" I explained as I grabbed the portafilter from his nervous hands.

"Thanks, Theo."

"Twist this here with your tamped grounds, then press this button."

"But how do you control how strong the shot is?" Sawyer asked.

"By the amount of water, you pull in proportion to the weight of the grounds."

"See! You learn something new every day!"

"I'll even tell Lord Perkins that you made this," I said.

"What if Lord Perkins wants another when you're not home?" Sawyer asked.

"Smash the machine, or cut the cord, or run to a local coffee shop. You gotta improvise, Chef!"

Sawyer began to have a full-blown laughing attack when I listed my terrible solutions. I loved making him laugh. It was always a goal of mine.

"I'll take this out to Lord Perkins. Maybe I'll try talking to him."

"No! I should!" Sawyer rebutted.

"No, relax!" I asserted.

"Theo, I should!"

"No."

"Fine, I'll fix you and your father some eggs and bacon. I'll be out in ten minutes."

"That sounds great, Chef. Thanks!" I smiled.

I carried my father's espresso and headed to the patio. He frequently sat on our stone patio. The patio looked like something from an ancient French château. The stone-slabbed ground supported two large wood pergolas over the long black iron dining set. It was the only piece of home my mother had here in Canada, the only piece of the house my father would allow. We had vines of grapes, something more of a decoration than an edible crop. The large grape leaves provided shade from the twelve hours of sun that spot received in the summer.

"Hey, morning," I said as I closed the patio door behind me.

"Morning, Theo," my father replied.

"I have your coffee."

"What? Why are you serving me? Do you not understand your role in this house? Perkins, do not serve!" my father barked.

"Sawyer tried to bring it out, but I snagged it from him."

"Well! I must have a word with Sawyer. This is unacceptable!" my father shouted.

"Really, I insisted!"

My father reached for his coffee with a look of sourness radiating from his chubby face. He was always so angry.

"Where's Mom?"

"Out!"

"Out where?"

"Out!"

"Yeah, but where?"

"Fuck! I told you Alexander! I mean Theodore!" my father screamed.

"Are you serious?" I replied.

"Your brother is usually the one trying to start fights with me!"

"Nobody is trying to fight you!" I rebutted.

"Alexander fights me every day!"

"You fight Alè every day!" I shot back.

"Are you kidding me? Fuck off!" my father screamed with a bloodshot face.

My father shot up from the iron table and pushed his chair back away from his body. He began to grunt, then began panting, taking louder breaths with every short inhale.

"I lost my cool. I didn't mean that Theodore!" my father explained with an embarrassed tone.

I had no words for my father. His disrespect deserved no response. As I turned around to re-enter the house, his fat body slammed back into the iron chair he had previously been sitting at.

"I love you," he grunted under his breath.

"Okay."

My father claiming to love me was nothing but guilt or an attempt to regain mental control of the situation. I shut the door behind me and grabbed my plate of eggs sitting on the counter.

"Our brunch date is cancelled. I'm eating in my room," I said to Sawyer.

"I'm sorry, kiddo."

"Don't be. I'm fine. Plus I gotta get ready. I'm going to Toronto today," I shouted as I stormed past Sawyer and then Alè.

I slammed my bedroom door behind me and shovelled my eggs down my throat while sitting in bed. I was considering, for the first time in my life, making Maria serve me in bed every morning going forward. I didn't want to make her work, but I also didn't want to eat with my father. I pondered whether I could buy a small two-seater table for Alè and me and put it in the corner of my room. Maybe one day, Alè and I could have our own apartment in the city, something like Wes', away from the other Perkins. Alè and Theo Dubois would make perfect roommates.

My phone lit up with a message from Wes. I was beyond excited to see his name again on my phone. Although we had only known each other for one day, I already had a massive crush on him.

Wes: *Hey T :) Still good for coffee before shopping?*

Theo: *DUH:)*

Wes: *Good :) See you at 1?*

Theo: *Sounds good Wes!*

I grabbed my things and headed down the stairs as I had planned to spend the day in Toronto, first with Wes, then all together with Jade and Wes. As I reached the bottom of the stairs, I realized I had nobody to take me to the train station. Maria had yet to return with my mother while she was off gallivanting with her Sicilian lover, so I had no options. My father was still home, but there was no way in hell I was going to sit in a car alone with him. He would've most likely started a fight over nothing and ended up throwing me out on the side of the highway, leaving me stranded with no other option but to stick my thumb out, hoping someone would pick me up. To my surprise, my father had been reading his paper at the dining room table next to Alè. They both sat in complete silence, no fighting, no screaming, just silence. Maybe he had exhausted his screaming capacity temporarily, as he had just had a verbal freakout about half an hour earlier on me.

"A little birdie told me you are headed to Toronto today!" my father said with a smile.

I looked over at Alè and slightly rolled my eyes as he was surely the 'little birdy' who had ratted me out.

"Yes."

"How are you getting there?" my father asked while holding his phoney smile.

I could see he felt guilty for yelling "fuck off" only a short while ago. I wasn't sure if he was actually feeling guilty or if he wanted to try to manipulate me with his fake smile to put me back under his control. The truth was, I saw through him. I was never under his control to begin with.

"I'm gonna order a ride on my phone, maybe."

"On your phone? That will surely cost you quite a lot from here, well, me quite a lot, since you children still leech off of our credit cards," my father said while cracking a large smile.

My father's light-hearted tone spoke for him. He most definitely was trying to ease his way back into being friendly without apologizing.

"I trust you, Theodore. Take my car!"

"Your car?"

"The McLaren!"

My eyes widened as I wasn't sure if I had been dreaming. Maybe this whole day hadn't happened yet. Maybe this was all a dream. That's why the energy felt so off.

"The-The—"

"Yes!"

"What? Why? Thanks!"

"I love you, that's why!" my father announced as his teeth reflected the light of the chandelier.

My brother and I glared at each other. I could see we were both as stunned. He began to mouth the words 'what the fuck' as I slightly smirked.

"Here!" my father announced as he tossed the keys at me.

I was never allowed to even look at my father's McLaren, let alone drive the thing. He had given me a brief lesson on how to drive the car, all verbal, of course, when he first brought her home. He referred to his car as a her. I had barely had my G2 permit for more than a few months, the permit that allowed me to drive without an adult present, so I was fairly inexperienced.

"I'll get her started for you. Come with me!"

I looked over my shoulder back at Alè. He was still in pure shock, as was I.

The interior garage door squeaked open as my father hopped in the driver's seat of his bright orange McLaren. The engine started and vibrated the whole garage. I loved the sound it made every time he started it.

"I'll see you later tonight. There's only one seat, so only one chick at a time, Theodore!" my father awkwardly joked.

"Are you sure?"

"Yup, enjoy!"

Archibald loved this car more than my mother, Alè, and myself combined. He must've felt really guilty. I sat down in the driver's seat and slowly inched out of the garage. My father, with Alè behind him, waved me off like the people of Southampton Port waved off the Titanic on her maiden voyage. I tapped the accelerator while leaving the driveway to test the car's power. She had a lot of it, almost too much for me to handle.

I flew down the old country roads, feeling more free than I had in a long time. The orange paint caught the glares of every passerby.

"Nice whip!" a group of teens hollered at me as I pulled up to a red light.

"Thanks."

"Daddy's money!" they yelled as they cackled while their driver pulled away.

I lived with that title my whole life, 'daddy's money.' I considered getting it tattooed on my arm as a joke, but I knew that it would not be well perceived by others. I hated labels, but I had always been labelled, so I learned to live with it.

I decided to not drive to the train station at all. I was going to drive directly to Toronto to show off my car to Wes. I was never one to show off, but had he been into cars, it was something that could spark up a conversation between us.

I drifted down the Gardiner Expressway and quickly exited the ramp in downtown Toronto. Every pedestrian practically broke their neck trying to catch a glimpse of my orange beauty. A few people even began to snap pictures on their phones, maybe to post on their social media. I also hated being the centre of attention, so this all felt foreign to me. I hated that everyone thought I was somehow more cool or valuable just because I was driving the orange beauty. I pulled up in front of the cafe Wes had texted me to meet at, catching one of the last street spots in front of the window. As I parked the car, I caught a glimpse of Wes sitting alone while staring out at the orange beauty. Then he jumped in pure shock as he realized it was me. As the door to the cafe swung open in front of me, I shuffled in to meet Wes at the table he had taken.

"Sorry, did you have to wait long for me?"

"Um, you're not gonna address the freaking McLaren you just casually rolled up in for coffee?" Wes giggled with excitement.

"Oh, that ol' thing."

"Mmm, Jade was right. You really are a royal prince!"

"Maybe."

"You're taking me for a spin after coffee. You have no choice," Wes demanded.

"Is that an order, Mr Creepy Instagram Stalker?" I asked with a grin.

"Duh!"

Both Wes and I began to laugh as he leaned in to hug me. Today he was wearing a completely different perfume. I couldn't put my finger on exactly what he had been wearing. His body perspired with the sweet smell of vanilla and bourbon. He smelled delicious.

"Do you drink flat whites?" Wes asked.

"Yes sir," I smirked.

"Mmm, seems about right."

"Mmm," I repeated.

Wes ordered the coffee while I sat down at the table. I kept staring at his beautiful body as he waited in line. His blond hair looked like silk in the lighting of the cafe. The way he politely interacted with the staff was a huge turn-on. I had a thing for people who treated others kindly. My family, aside from Alè and I, treated staff and people of a lesser status in society than themselves like absolute shit. If I was ever going to date someone, kindness was a necessity. His skinny shoulders held his posture back perfectly aligned. I could tell Wes was active. His body appeared to be in perfect physical shape. I was never one to care about muscles for myself, but it was a trait I found so very attractive in guys.

"They kinda fucked up these flat whites. They look like regular lattes," Wes said with an ounce of defeat in his voice.

"Prob still tastes good," I shot back.

"Hopefully!"

I took one sip of the coffee. It tasted of burnt tar and slightly off-date milk.

"Wow!" I said in a shocked tone.

"This tastes like shit. I'm sorry, T, I misled us here."

"Don't be sorry. I'm just happy to be with you." I smiled.

"Mmm, victims always fall in love with their stalkers. I guess my plan worked then," Wes said.

"In love? Slow down, Wessy baby," I said.

"Wessy sounds like an STD!"

We both began to hysterically laugh so loud that it grabbed the attention of the whole cafe. Wes practically spit his burnt coffee all over the table but quickly blocked his mouth with his hand. Our energy was intertwined. We just understood each other in a way I had never been understood in my whole life.

"Let's go for a drive. The vibes and coffee are not great in here," I said while looking around the room.

"I thought you would never ask, shit!"

We grabbed our things and tossed the six-dollar burnt lattes at the door. I felt bad that Wes had wasted twelve dollars on such awful coffee, but he didn't seem too bothered.

"This can't be yours, like I'm still shook you have one of these!"

"It's my father's car."

"I've never seen one in person, like never."

"Well, now you get to see and ride in one."

We both hopped in my father's McLaren. I could tell Wes was in awe as he sunk his butt down into the seat. His head spun on a swivel while he took in the whole interior. As the engine fired up, he giddied like a little boy. I found his excited little yelp the cutest thing I had ever heard. I loved that he was in pure bliss.

"Ready, Wessy?"

"Gun it!"

We slowly peeled out of the street parking spot. I had to be careful of the busy city surrounding us. We drove around the whole downtown core while Wes smiled from ear to ear. I loved making him smile. It made him even more beautiful. His teeth were perfectly straight, shining like pearls from my mother's personal collection. I did a few circles around the downtown core before I drove down to the waterfront harbour.

As I turned onto Lakeshore Boulevard, I wanted to impress Wes and attempted to perform a slight drift. I didn't know what came over me. I was behaving like a complete fool in front of him. I accelerated hard and tapped the brakes attempting to drift the orange beauty into the turn I was taking. It was a stupid idea, a horrendous idea even. The front end of the orange beauty spun, and the rear lost complete control sending us in the direct path of a utility pole.

The rear tires spun as the right side of the car drifted closer to the wood pole as we slid over the curb and onto the sidewalk. By some miracle, we didn't collide with the utility pole. Wes' eyes went from cheerful to fearful in a matter of one nanosecond. I hated that I scared him. It gutted me.

"I-I am so sorry!"

"Holy shit!"

"Wes, please forgive me. That was so stupid, FUCK!"

"I didn't know I was in the presence of Vin Diesel!" Wes said with a smile.

I started to giggle, which cut through the tension inside the car.

"Vin is kinda hot, like in an older type of way."

"Mmm."

"What? You don't agree?" I asked.

"No, I do. It's just that I think you have a thing for older guys. Maybe that's why you like me, then." Wes asserted with a flirty grin.

"You're barely a year older," I said. "Who said I liked you?"

"Mmm."

"Who?" I said with a smile.

Wes silenced my flirtatious demands with his pointer finger. He silenced my mouth by placing his finger across my lips. His eyes widened then he immediately shut them. As he began to lean in, he grabbed my neck with his left hand. He opened his eyes as he got closer to my face. Initially, he didn't kiss me as expected. His sapphire-blue eyes directed their gaze into mine. I felt an immediate inner warmth like his eyes lit an internal flame inside of me. My palms began to sweat as his strong gaze gave me slight anxiety. Our lips interlocked as his sapphire eyes shielded behind his eyelids. His kiss tasted of a slight hint of peppermint. He must've been chewing gum after our terrible coffees because it tasted so fresh, like he had never sipped on the coffee in the first place. As I leaned back, he pulled me in for another thirty seconds before we both took a pause.

"Shit!"

"Shit," he imitated under his breath.

"Well, that was hot."

"Hotter than hot, Prince T."

"HEY, ASSHOLE, GET OFF THE SIDEWALK!" We heard as we both turned our heads to see an angry pedestrian tapping the passenger window.

Both Wes and I began to scream our heads off. I had never laughed so hard in the eighteen years I had been alive. I quickly tapped the accelerator and shot the orange beauty back onto the road.

The whole ride to the mall to meet Jade, both Wes and I mocked the line "HEY, ASSHOLE!" while breaking into severe laughter each time one of us said it. Wes and I now had an inside joke. I had known him for less than two days, and we had already made out, been to a show together, and had an inside joke. I loved the rate at which our relationship was progressing.

CHAPTER FIVE

Wes and I pulled into the parking garage of the Eaton Centre. Jade texted me that she had already been waiting downstairs on the lower level, ordering herself her notorious Vanilla Bean Frappuccino from Starbucks. She drank one every day in place of the typical coffee that practically everyone else drank. Jade hated coffee but still wanted to feel like she fit in with the coffee crowd.

As we rode the escalator down to the lower floor, I caught a glimpse of Jade's familiar curly locks of brown hair from behind. She turned around as Wes called her name from the escalator. Jade's face was that of excitement with a hint of slight embarrassment from being called across the sea of hundreds of Torontonians strolling the lower level of the mall. Her embarrassment quickly turned into curiosity as she noticed Wes and I had come in together. She gave me a slight wink as to insinuate she knew about Wes and me.

"Jade!" Wes announced again as we approached the Starbucks line.

"Hey, guys!"

"Frap o'clock?" I said with a smile.

"You bet! Do you guys want anything?"

"Nah, I'm on coffee number four today," Wes said.

"So, y'all been hanging out before this?"

"Psh, no. I met this guy in the hallway by chance," I pleaded as beads of sweat formed on my hairline.

"Yeah, I saw T's big head in the crowd of people, and I flagged him down!" Wes added.

I awkwardly laughed as Wes stared me down. We both couldn't conceal the child-like giggling. Jade knew we were both full of it. Her eyes showed her unwillingness to believe.

"I have to buy a gift for Kate. She's flying from Spain tonight!" Jade said, trying to change the subject.

"Where was Kate? Like what part of Spain?" I inquired.

"Mallorca!"

"So pretty!" Wes added.

Kate was Jade's older sister. She was the more adventurous sibling. Kate spent time in many countries around the world working as a flight attendant. She was always in some random location, living it up like the globetrotter she was. Jade much preferred to stay in Canada, a homebody in contrast.

"What are you gonna get her?" I asked.

"Dunno, maybe a cute shirt or something," Jade said.

"Yeah, but how do you know her size?" Wes asked.

"She's my sister. I know her size plus she's thin, she fits into anything!" Jade said with a slight tone of resentment.

Kate was very skinny, almost skinnier than Alè. Jade's father always compared them, which tore at Jade's confidence. Jade was slightly heavier than her sister, which always made her feel slightly inferior to her. I hated that Jade felt this way. She was drop-dead gorgeous. As her gay best friend, I knew she would land a hot model boyfriend one day.

We strolled the shops along the bottom level of the mall, making our way through each of them. After a few hours of running up and down the levels, Jade finally began her hunt for her sister's shirt. We had completely forgotten to search for one as we got sidetracked about twelve times.

My pocket began to vibrate violently so I stepped out of the store and into the hallway. I pulled my phone out to see I had three missed calls from Maria. I didn't typically receive phone calls from Maria, not in the middle of the day, especially when she knew I was out. As I dialed Maria's number, my mind began to race. I couldn't help but think my family had been in a fiery crash or someone had been attacked. Every possible bad scenario that could've happened snowballed in my anxious brain.

"Maria?" I barked.

"Theo, mijo," Maria sobbed.

"No! Why do you sound like that?"

"Theo!" she choked.

"Tell me, Maria!"

"Theo, everything is okay, love. Nobody is hurt!"

"Okay, so what's up?" I asked.

"Theo, Alexander has been admitted to the hospit—"

"I thought you said that—" I yelled as Maria cut in.

"He's okay! He needed to visit." Maria said with a slight sniffle.

"What? Why?"

"Your brother was taken to the emergency room, mijo."

"The emergency room?"

"Yes, I'm here with him, I brought him some coffee, and I'm keeping him company."

"Maria, what hospital? Oakville?"

"Yes."

I hung up on her abruptly. I didn't mean to be rude. I was not thinking critically.

I stormed over to Jade and Wes, who had been looking through shirts for Jade's sister, and bombarded them with the information I just learned.

"I'm coming with you, T!" Wes declared.

"No, stay," I replied. "Keep Jade company."

"I have to go soon, Theo. My sister flies home in about two hours. I'm only going to see her for a few days cuz she's taking another flight," Jade reminded me.

"You're not going alone, T!" Wes said.

"Okay," I whimpered.

Both Jade and Wes hugged me then we said our goodbyes to Jade. Wes and I began sprinting through the hallways of the Eaton Center, practically tossing other shoppers out of our path.

We pulled out of the parking garage attached to the mall, drifting around each downtown block until we hit the highway. Once I hit the highway, I allowed the orange beauty to open up. Her engine purred, and the front end raised as we soared down the Gardiner Expressway. Wes put his hand on my knee, his way of comforting me in a moment of despair. I knew I shouldn't have been driving, Wes would have been a better choice, but it was too late now.

Wes and I barely spoke until we hit Mississauga, the city between Toronto and Oakville. Wes could sense I was too tense to strike up a light-hearted conversation. After about fifteen minutes, he finally broke the silence.

"Are you okay?"

"Don't ask me that."

"I-I'm sor—"

"Fuck, no, I'm sorry! I know you care," I cut in while caressing his hand on my knee.

"You don't owe me an apology, Theo."

"I didn't mean to be snappy with you."

Wes squeezed my hand as his sapphire eyes locked down on me.

"It's gonna be okay, T."

"I dunno."

"It is."

We pulled into the parking garage of the hospital in Oakville. Oakville was the town just south of rural Milton. We did have a hospital in Milton. However, the hospital in Oakville was about the same distance from Perkins Palace. I had no idea what state my brother was in or if he even wanted visitors, but I didn't care. I was going to see my brother, or I was not leaving. Security would have had to drag me out by my toes if they wanted me out. Even then, I'd still put up a fight. Maria had sent me the room number in a text message, assuming I was coming to the hospital as I had dramatically hung up on her about an hour ago.

As Wes and I approached the room, I heard Maria's soft, motherly voice hum the children's folk song called *Una Mariposita* she sang to Alè and me as little boys when she put us to sleep. The ancient song was about a small butterfly. That's all I understood with my very limited Spanish knowledge. For all I knew, Maria could have been cursing us out. It didn't make much sense in English when she translated it, but in Spanish, it sounded beautiful. We both waited outside the door and let her finish her lullaby.

After Maria's song concluded, Wes motioned for me to go in while he waited for me in the hallway to not intrude on the intimate moment.

"Hi," I whispered in a soft tone.

Both Maria and Alè's heads spun towards the entrance of the room where I was standing. Maria had been caressing Alè's cheeks while she ran her other hand through his chocolate-coloured hair. Alè looked embarrassed but also half excited to see me. I could tell they had him on some strong medications as his eyes were half shut, and he appeared to be mentally out of it.

"Come here, mijo!" Maria ordered with a smile.

As I approached the bed, I saw Maria's thumb gently rubbing the back of Alè's hand. He was crying from Maria's lullaby, a song she whispered to us in bed when we refused to sleep as children.

"I'm sorry," Alè whimpered.

"For what?"

"Scaring you."

"I'm still scared Alè. What happened?"

"I just got a little anxious, that's all."

I could see in Alè's face I knew that so much more had happened. He was a terrible liar.

"Theo, can I have a word?" Maria asked as she motioned for me to step outside.

I followed Maria outside of the hospital room, about six feet from the door. Wes had grabbed a seat about five doors down and smiled at me as I caught his glance.

"Your father, he—" Maria began to explain as I cut her off.

"What did he do to Alè?"

"THEO!"

63

"What did he do?"

"Your father has employed me for years, Theo. In all of those years, I have never seen him behave the way he did this afternoon."

"Maria, what did he do?"

Maria began to tremble as her eyes became saturated with tears.

"Maria, please! Tell me!" I pleaded.

"Well, you see, Alexander and your father got into a fight after you left. I don't know how it started, but it was a bad fight, Theo! Your father shoved your poor brother into the wall in the front foyer!"

"Shoved him? He put his fat hands on my brother?" I shrieked as a ball of rage grew large inside my stomach.

"Yes," Maria cried. "Then he told your brother he was better off dead as he was a burden to the whole family. Alexander went upstairs and—he-he—swallowed a whole bottle of pills but later called an ambulance, realizing what he had done. I waited for the medics to arrive, and I followed them here," Maria explained in tears.

"Where is that fat fuck now?" I demanded.

"At home, he didn't want to come."

"Didn't want to come?" I repeated.

"No, Theo, no."

"Where's my mother, still out?" I asked.

"She hasn't come back from her friend's house."

"Her boyfriend's house," I corrected, shaking my head in disgust.

I began to uncontrollably cry as I fell to my knees. Had Alè not called the medics, the pills would have taken him this afternoon. I was still in complete shock as I rested on my knees on the cold hospital floor. Maria rushed back in to comfort my half-sleeping brother. As I stood up, Wes' arms held me up then he quickly hugged me. His soul knew mine was hurting, even if he couldn't understand the reason why with his lack of knowledge of the situation. As Wes held me, a nurse pushed past us and told Maria she had to leave for the evening because Alè needed to rest from his recent stomach pump. Maria refused to leave my brother's side. She might as well have been admitted as well.

"I think we should go."

"Are you sure? I don't mind waiting if you want to go spend some time with your brother."

"No, it's okay. He should get some sleep. He has had a rough day, Wes," I explained.

I waved at Maria and Alè, but my brother was already in a deep sleep. He looked like he was in a coma, dead almost. I couldn't bear the site. I needed to get out of the hospital.

Wes and I hopped back in the orange beauty as I instructed Wes to take over as the DJ.

"No sad shit," I pleaded.

Wes started blasting pop music as we screamed the lyrics like it was karaoke night at a local dive bar. He made fun of my scratchy voice as I tried to sing on-pitch while failing miserably. I desperately needed the distraction of Wes. My mind was fighting with every ounce of power it had to not focus on the fact my brother had attempted to take his own life this afternoon. I was so far in denial that I was essentially gaslighting myself that none of this was my reality. Deep down, I understood it was.

"Thank you," I blurted to break the silence.

"Mmm, for what, T?" Wes asked.

"For coming!" I replied as I turned down Wes' music.

"You seemed like you needed someone. I could sense it," he added with a smile.

"Yeah."

"I don't know your family well, but I feel like I know you a little bit now."

"HA! If you have the time, maybe I'll put together a slideshow with two hundred slides and present it to you. Then maybe, just maybe, you will be up to speed with my crazy life," I said.

"I would attend the entire lecture and even take notes." Wes grinned.

I knew he was serious. He was so into me that I could feel he was not the slightest bit joking. Talking with him, having him here on one of the darkest days of my life thus far was a blessing. I felt at home with him, despite knowing him for such a short period of time.

"I'll take you home. It's getting late."

"You can drop me off at one of the train stations. I can take the train back."

"Are you kidding? After how much you were there for me today, I'm not gonna drop you off at some station and peel away like some jerk," I said.

"A true gentleman you are, T."

"Yes sir!"

I looked over at Wes. His eyes sparkled with pure adoration with a slight sparkle of pity. I knew I was safe, a feeling missing from my chaotic life.

I pulled up to the front door of Wes' building on King Street West. He turned over to thank me for the drive home, but I stopped him mid-sentence.

"I should be thanking you!" I shot back.

"No, seriously, I'm glad I could be there."

"Hopefully, this date wasn't too chaotic. Hopefully, we can go on a second!"

"Well, it was slightly chaotic, but I love chaos!"

"Oh, then it's meant to be!" I said.

Wes slightly chuckled, then silenced me with a swift kiss. His lips wrapped around mine as a way of politely silencing my anxious rambling.

"Bye, T."

"Bye," I shot back with an affectionate doe-eyed gaze.

As I drove back to the Perkins Palace, my mind began to unfreeze. All of the distractions that Wes had provided faded into the abyss of nothingness before my eyes. I was flooded with over fifty emotions at once. Anger, sadness, disbelief, disgust, fear, horror, and many more. They all hit me like a semi-truck strikes a deer crossing the highway in the night. I wanted to vomit, scream, and cry all simultaneously. The fact my father had the nerve to say those ungodly words to my brother, especially knowing of his delicate mental health, was one of the most deplorable things Archibald had ever done. I had zero respect for my father now. Every shred of it disintegrated. If anyone was "better off dead," it was Archibald. Archibald was always the problem in our family. The thought of him passing his crown of blame upon my brother made me physically ill. Alè was not to blame. He never was.

As children, Archibald began singling my brother out, constantly making him feel subpar to me. He saw Alè as the "weaker brother," the brother with less courage and Perkins pride. I was never overly coura-geous, but my father had a twisted internal illusion that I was.

One winter, we took a ski trip to Big White in Kelowna, a ski resort in the Rockies. Alè had torn his knee while attempting a jump. We had both done this jump about fifty times that weekend, but for whatever reason, Alè twisted the wrong way on his landing. After the crash, he was unable to walk properly, so I had a ski medic called in to escort him to the ski-side medical clinic for an assessment.

His knee was torn, but the bones were not broken, according to the nurses running the clinic. They instruct-ed that Alè was to rest for a few days before we could have him assessed at the hospital, as my father had planned to stay at the resort for the remainder of the trip. I could tell my brother was in excruciating pain as he let out a gasp every time he had to walk between the bath-room and kitchen of our ski chalet. He was in no condi-tion to walk, never mind skiing, but my father did not believe so. He constantly disregarded Alè's injury and repeated that he was "too much of a sissy" because he refused to leave the living room couch.

My father picked on Alè the entire trip afterwards. He made Alè cry a few times as he slapped the injury with his fat, mallet-like claws he called hands. My brother begged multiple times for my father to stop antagonizing him, but his face showed no remorse. I could have done more, but instead, I allowed my father to treat Alè like human garbage. That ski trip solidified for me that my father lacked basic human empathy. His brain did not have such an ability pre-installed in its hard drive.

One summer, we visited Lac d'Annecy, France, staying with family friends nearby. My father's friend, Gabriel, who owned the house at which we were staying, wanted to take us out on his grandfather's old wooden runabout boat. Gabriel, my father, Alè, and I packed into his forty-year-old runabout, a small honey-glazed wooden boat with a brown leather bench that had seating for just the men on board. We practically sat shoulder-to-shoulder, especially because my father's fat body pressed both my brother and me up against the sides. About halfway into our ride, we had been cruising through the middle of the lake.

My father screamed up to Gabriel, who had been driving us around, "Wanna see a sissy swim?" as he grabbed Alè by the shirt and tossed him directly into the lake in one swift movement. My brother was not a strong swimmer, and the action caught him off guard. He began to thrash and panic in the middle of the lake like the helpless, drowning child that he was. I instantly threw my body off of the back of the boat as I realized what my father had done in an attempt to entertain our host. I was a stronger swimmer than Alè, ten times practically.

I cut through the water like an Olympic athlete as the adrenaline kicked in as I made my way to my brother's rescue. I dragged Alè back towards the boat as he began to scold my father like he was a small child. All of Alè's scolding was disregarded with my father's evil laughter. Alè practically tore the French flag off of its mast while scrambling to get back in the boat. The whole ride back to the shore, neither Alè nor I said a word to my father.

He attempted to tell us multiple times that he was "just playing," but drowning your oldest son was not a game.

I looked back on that day on Lac d'Annecy and regret not sticking up for my brother more. My father loved to pick on Alè at the expense of his son's own self-worth and mental health. I never told my mother what had happened. I cowered down to my father and let him uphold the dynamic of power in the situation.

CHAPTER SIX

I rolled over to see my phone had two paragraphs awaiting my response, one from Jade and one from Wes. I opened Jade's storybook of a text, something she rarely sent as most of our texts were brief and to the point. Nothing was to be taken rudely from our short conversations. That was just how we texted one another.

Jade: *Hey Theo, I hope ur doing alright love. I heard about Alè from Wes. He didn't rly tell me much about what happened cuz he said he wanted u to tell me in person no matter how hard I pressed him. I also wanted to say like dude it's totally cool if ur seeing Wes. Like I kinda got the vibes when we were at the Eaton Centre and the way Wes talks about u I can tell hes obsessed. I'm not mad at you love. I want u to know that. I don't think Wes or I ever had the same vibe y'all do together like I'm rly happy for u. Keep me updated on Alè. Call me tn? <3*

Theo: *Hey Jade! Thank you love! I will keep you updated on Alè. Also yes I rly like him. Like I really really like him. I'm sorry if this is weird for u. Love u lots, lets call sometime soon <3*

I closed my phone as I unpacked Jade's message. I never intended for any of this to happen. I knew she liked Wes, but I couldn't help the connection we had. I then remembered Wes also sent me a long paragraph.

Wes: *Hey T. So uh Jade had been on me about us. I didn't know what to tell her. She is like a judge in court holy shit like I couldn't hide nothing from her, like even over text! I didn't tell her about us, whatever we are haha.*

Also, idk what Maria said to u yesterday but you looked rly sad which was hard to see. I don't wanna snoop into the details but if u ever wanna talk about stuff, I'm here T :)

Also, do u wanna grab a movie tn downtown? My treat <3

Theo: *Hey Wessy :) I don't think we gotta keep it from Jade. I told her I like you. Its prol gonna be awkward for a bit ahhhh. But I really like u <3*

I think Alè might be coming home today. I wanna be here to greet him when he gets home. Lets reschedule, I wanna see u tho :)

As soon as I sent the message, Wes reacted to the message with a heart. He replied about five seconds later.

Wes: *Of course T :) I can't wait to see u.*

Also…shittttt Prince T has balls!

I wasn't sure if they would be releasing Alè today or if it would be later on in the week. I wanted to be here in case they did. I also needed to unpack my emotions and set them aside. There wasn't room in this massive home for two unwell people. I was Alè's main support, and I was not going to let him down. As I got dressed, another message came in, this time from Maria.

Maria: *Hey Theo. We're coming home! We will be there in an hour.*

Theo: *See you guys soon <3*

I grabbed my things and headed down to the kitchen to make myself my regular morning espresso. Neither my father nor my mother were anywhere to be seen. I checked the garage to see my father's daily driver had been absent from its regular spot. My mother's car was also missing from the garage. My father's absence made sense. He had a lot to be ashamed of, given how the events of his last interaction with Alè played out. He was most likely hiding amongst his greaseball friends, either with Dom or some goon of equivalent status.

I shut the garage door as I overheard Sawyer preparing breakfast for me in the kitchen. He must've heard me awake and wanted to prepare me something special. I feared he was taking pity on me for everything I had been through with Alè. I absolutely hated when people did things out of pity, although I was unsure of his intentions because preparing breakfast was his job.

"No coffee shop runs required. I'm here to work the machine!" I said as I stepped into the kitchen.

"Good morning Theo," Sawyer said with a smile.

"Whatcha making?"

"Your fave. Banana pancakes with Belgian milk chocolate between the layers!"

I knew now that he was most definitely taking pity on me.

"Oh, you don't have to."

"Already started, Theo. Take a seat," he said as he pointed towards the breakfast nook around the corner where I typically ate my toast with jam at. Toast with jam was about all that I had the skill set to make.

"Thank you, Chef. It means a lot."

"Did you sleep alright?" Sawyer asked.

"Chef, I think I napped for about forty minutes." I said as my eyes drifted down to the floor.

I could tell Sawyer regretted asking me how I had slept. It was quite obvious that when your brother attempted to end his life by swallowing a bottle of old prescription drugs just the day before, sleep was not something that was going to come easy.

"I'm sorry—I should not have ask—"

"No! Ask away. I'm glad you care about me." I smiled.

"I do care about you, kid, a lot, actually."

I smiled at Sawyer, then quickly turned to the espresso machine as I had forgotten to pull my shot.

"I practised a bit last night, but I still think you're the master, Theo!"

"You practised? That is the cutest thing ever, Chef!"

Sawyer began to smile. You could see the pride radiating from his well-structured face. He was a good-looking man. Had he not been a personal chef, he may have been successful trying his luck at a modelling agency in Milan or Paris.

"So, what did you see yesterday?" I asked as Sawyer stacked the final pancake.

"See? Everything Theo. Every. Single. Thing."

"Please don't spare the details of Lord Perkins' rage," I pleaded. "You are safe to tell me everything."

"Okay. Let me just finish garnishing these pancakes, then I'll tell you what I witnessed."

"Make some for yourself too!"

"What?"

"Yeah! Have breakfast with me, Chef."

"Oh, but Theo, you know what would happen if your father saw me eating with you? I'm not supposed to dine with the family members such as yourself."

"HA! Fuck him and his rules. You are not my servant. We are equals, Chef," I said. "Now plate yourself some pancakes while I pour you a macchiato. That's your favourite, right?"

Sawyer's eyes practically had tears in them. He had never been treated like a human in this god-awful place I called home. I hated that my father ingrained into his head that he didn't matter. He was a dirty kitchen servant who had to bend over backwards for every command that left my father's mouth. I saw Sawyer as a good man, one that deserved every ounce of respect that was lacking from his life here.

Sawyer returned to the breakfast nook about five minutes after serving me my pancakes. The breakfast nook was just far enough from the kitchen that you couldn't fully see the person sitting there but close enough that you could openly converse with their half-visible silhouette.

"You-you—"

"I waited for you, yes." I interrupted as he stood there dumbfounded. "Your coffee is piping hot, just for you, sir."

"Theo, here, switch pancakes with me. You take the hot ones!" Sawyer insisted.

"Nope! Those are yours. You take the hot ones, Chef!"

"No, Theo, really, please I don't want to ruin your breakfast."

I licked the pancakes like a little child would to claim their territory. Sawyer chuckled at my childish notion.

"Now you gotta eat the hot ones," I declared.

Sawyer sat down and began to slice up his pancakes. I could tell he was nervous about dining with me like he'd been in the presence of The King of England or The President of The United States. My father made all of the people who worked for us to see us as such, although we were not.

"So, what happened yesterday?"

"I don't even know where to start."

"Take your time. My brother won't be home for about an hour."

"He's coming back today?"

"Yeah, apparently, they released him."

Sawyer seemed shocked that Alè was coming home so suddenly. I wasn't overly shocked. Our mental health system was severely broken in Canada. Although my brother may have been physically stable after his stomach pump, he most definitely needed to be under close supervision still.

"I was filleting the yellowfin tuna for last night's appetizer when your father and Alexander began to argue over the volume of the show your brother had been watching in the TV den. The show was fairly loud, but I didn't mind it as it kept me entertained as I worked."

"Let me guess, my father started the argument," I added.

"Uh, well, you see—"

"Don't hold back!" I cut in.

"Yes. He did," Sawyer said with fearful eyes.

"Thank you."

"Anyways, as your father asked your brother to turn the show down. Your brother calmly told him it was going to be over in two minutes. The show was not too loud, a normal volume, really. Well, your father did not take that well. He went into the garage and grabbed a wrench that must've been sitting out on the workbench. He then beat the wrench violently into the display then tossed the wrench onto the ground. Alexander obviously lost his cool and for good reason!" Sawyer said. "He then followed your father and confronted his behaviour which turned into a full-blown screaming match in the front foyer. If I'm being fully transparent, Maria and I contemplated calling the police to break up the fight, as it was the worst we had ever seen in the time we had worked here. We both decided not to, as we knew our employment would end the moment we called. Your father then proceeded to get so heated that he picked Alexander up and threw him into the drywall using his full strength. Alexander did not stand a chance. He was unable to physically defend himself. As your father left the foyer, your brother told him he wished he was never born into this psychotic family, to which your father then replied that if that's how he felt, he was better off dead. I felt terrible for not intervening, Theo. I am so sorry!"

I sat in silence for a few moments trying to gather my thoughts.

"Chef, none of that was your fault. I understand why you didn't jump in," I said in an attempt to comfort Sawyer.

"I'm a coward. You don't understand. I'm a coward!" Sawyer said as his eyes welled in tears.

"I do understand. I have been you, the bystander of Archibald's madness and bullying. I understand."

"I should have jumped in, being the only person here capable of physically defending your brother!" Sawyer cried.

"Don't be too hard on yourself. Thank you for telling me the truth. I know that wasn't easy."

Sawyer and I finished our pancakes in silence as we cleared our dishes from the breakfast nook. He refused to let me wash my own plate, despite how many times I insisted. After my time in the kitchen concluded, I walked over to the den to verify Sawyer's story. It wasn't that I didn't believe Sawyer. I did. I just had to investigate the evidence for myself. As I approached the den, I noticed the TV mount was bare where the TV once sat flush against the wall. I wouldn't have been surprised if a replacement was going to arrive in a brown cardboard box at the front gates this afternoon. I was almost certain this would happen.

I walked over to the front foyer where my father had thrown my brother into the wall, and to my surprise, the wall had been slightly dented in an Alè sized silhouette. Feeling the dent brought tears to my eyes. If he was capable of this from one argument over a TV, he was capable of so much more. My family was in grave danger from the person who was supposed to lead it. The man who was supposed to be the reigning Perkins sovereign.

The door swung open as Maria led my brother in by his right arm.

"Hi, Theo," Alè mumbled with a slight tone of embarrassment.

I wrapped my arms around my brother, tightening my grip with every exhale of his chest.

"Okay, don't suffocate me now, asshole," he said.

"Now there's my Alè!"

I took my brother's things and set them down in the front den. He made his way to the kitchen to greet Sawyer.

"Can I get you anything, Alexander?" Sawyer inquired.

"Actually, an espresso would be lovely if you don't mind."

Sawyer looked at me with a slight grin.

"C'mon, Chef, you said you had been practising!" I said.

"Coming up!"

I watched Sawyer struggle slightly to get the machine working, but after about thirty seconds, he remembered his practice sessions and the operation became smooth, almost professional looking.

"Alè, come on a walk with me after your coffee. I wanna talk."

"No, I want to check over my gear. Tom and I may go fishing or something in Muskoka."

"You are not going anywhere!"

"I want to go up north!"

"That's great, but you're staying here."

"Talk about this outside."

Maria appeared to be in complete shock that Alè had uncovered his plans to go on a fishing trip with Tom. If Tom showed up at the house attempting to take my brother away, I was going to slash his truck tires. Nobody gets in, nobody gets out until I know my brother is safe. If I had to hand-dig a ten-foot-wide alligator-infested moat surrounding Perkins Palace, I was going to do it. If Alè was going to his room, so was I. If Alè was going to eat, so was I. If Alè was going to the washroom, I was going to stand behind him while he urinated. He lost his privilege of privacy, one that he would not earn back from me until I felt he was safe.

Alè finished his coffee then I dragged him out to the meadow for a private conversation. I selected a spot we used to converse as little boys, a small shaded area of tall grass under a large sugar maple tree. The tree looked about four hundred years old. It had been here longer than the Perkins dynasty had been and would be here four hundred years after the Perkins dynasty fell.

"I used to love this spot. All of the shit we talked about people here, the gossip tree we used to call it." Alè chuckled in a light-hearted tone.

"Yeah, mostly gossip about Archibald The Evil."

"Evil he is."

"I-I heard—" I began to mumble. "I heard about what happened."

"He looked like he was capable of killing me. I was so scared, Theo!" Alè sobbed as he buried his head into my shoulder.

"I'd kill him first!"

"You can't always be there!" he shouted.

I held my brother's hand to calm him down.

"His eyes rolled sideways, like a great white hunting seals! He wanted my blood!"

Alè began to hyperventilate as he recalled the events of the day prior. I placed my hand firmly on his sternum.

"Breathe," I whispered. "Breathe."

Alè began to calm down enough that I could once again begin to reason with him. I hated seeing what my father did to him. Archibald could have been in Spain at the moment for all I knew, but his presence still lingered fresh in my brother's energy field.

"You're not going fishing, you know that right."

"I know, Theo, I know."

I began to sob as I realized my brother was correct earlier. I couldn't always be there, despite my intentions to.

"I'm sorry I wasn't there yesterday," I whimpered.

"It's not your fault!" Alè said with a stern glare.

"It feels like it is."

"It's not!" Alè shouted.

"I know."

Alè and I laid on our backs and watched the clouds pass by through the branches, an activity we did under this exact tree years ago.

"Look! That one looks like Maria!" Alè laughed.

"Holy shit! I see it!"

"Remember when she would practically spy on us as kids then report us to Mom?"

"Maria was like a walking security system. She knew everyone's business," I said.

"Yeah! When I first started dating Skylar, Mom already knew that girl's birthday, height, and Social Insurance Number before I had the chance to introduce her."

I began to slightly chuckle as I turned to see Alè laughing with a slight spec of sadness from the raw memories of Skylar's traumatic departure from his life.

"Alè!" I blurted.

"What?"

"Please promise me something. No matter how bad things get, you will never swallow a bottle of pills ever again." I cried.

Alè began to stare off into the distance like he was searching the realms of the universe for an appropriate response to my demand.

"I will never swallow a bunch of pills again," he mumbled under his breath.

"I love you." I whispered.

"I love you too, Theo."

We laid in silence for about half an hour, watching the passing clouds and birds swoop across the tree line. I knew this was exactly what Alè needed, some alone time with his brother.

His aura radiated peace, a feeling he rarely got to experience. I needed this, too, more than my brother ever knew.

The evening came, and neither my mother nor my father returned home. Maybe now was the best time to excavate my moat, to keep my father out permanently. Maria helped Sawyer prepare a traditional Puerto Rican dish she called 'mofongo.' It was essentially a mashed plantain bed with crispy pork skin. It sounded like a delicacy the way she described it. My father always forbade what he called "ethnic food." When he was home, we typically dined on dishes that were more European in nature. I enjoyed being adventurous with foods, especially delicious dishes from the Caribbean. I got the feeling this was essentially Maria's form of a micro-protest, even if my father was absent from tonight's dinner.

Maria called us down for dinner as Alè and I were listening to some old rock records from my collection. I still refused to let him out of my sight, so I didn't care if he'd prefer to do something else. We were joined at the hip going forward.

As we walked down to the dining room, only two plates had been set out.

"Maria! What is this?" I announced across the whole main level.

Maria summoned herself from the den where she had been bringing over the silverware for Alè and me.

"Is everything alright, Theo?" Maria asked.

"No, this is all wrong!" I said with a smile.

"Oh, I—"

"Where's yours and Chef Sawyer's plates?" I asked. "Oh, and grab one for David too. I'll fetch him from the garden."

"What?"

"Yeah, tonight we eat as a family!" I announced.

"Theo, I am not allowed to dine with you and your brother, you know this," Maria explained with a puzzled complexion. "Your father he—"

"Mmm, last time I checked, my father is missing at the moment, which makes me King of the castle."

"HA! I'm actually older, so that makes ME King of the castle!" Alè interjected.

"Steal my crown, why don't you?"

Alè smiled at my sarcastic remark.

"As King, I command all persons, far and wide, to eat together at once!" Alè said.

"You heard the king, now fetch some plates while I fetch David."

Maria looked absolutely stunned. Sawyer was fond of this idea, as I'd already broken the rules with him in secrecy not more than a few hours ago.

I walked out into the garden to find David had been applying fertilizer to the potted boxwoods my father loved to show off when guests came around. David had them shaped into a perfect cube at my father's request, an ode to his rigid personality as I saw it.

"Hey!"

"Hello, Mr Perkins!" David smiled.

"David, you don't have to call me that. Theo works for me!" I corrected.

"Sorry, my apologies, Theo."

David dropped the bag of synthetic fertilizer as I began to invite him in for dinner. He looked the most confused out of all of them. David had only been in the main house maybe five times in his life. He was what my father considered an "outside man."

"I-I-I don't understand."

"C'mon, dinner is gonna get cold!" I smiled.

David followed me at a slow pace. It was obvious how foreign the interior of the house felt to him. He looked up in awe at the crystal chandeliers and oil paintings that were scattered across each room, stopping at each like a student on an art trip in the city.

I pulled out David's chair and asked him to take his seat. Maria looked mortified that I, Theo Perkins, was seating David, the exterior property maintenance man. Both Maria and Sawyer looked afraid to sit down at their seats.

"Theo, what if your father comes home?" Maria asked.

"Since when are you afraid of Arch?" I said.

The whole room erupted in genuine laughter, a missing component from all dinners we had at this table prior.

"I love this silverware! I don't think I've used stuff this nice before!" David proclaimed.

"Great job on the—" Alè froze.

"Mofongo."

"Mofongo, yes!" Alè repeated. "Thanks, Maria."

The chatter in the room began to pick up as time progressed. I could tell Maria, Sawyer, and David all appeared to be enjoying their meals, especially since they rarely ate complete meals without my parents interrupting them to bring them some tea or to run them a hot bath or some other ridiculous task. My parents were both helpless, like two toddlers in adult bodies. I never understood how they didn't feel embarrassed to rely on them so often.

"We should do this more often!" I said as I looked around the room.

"Arch would have to kick the bucket before this became a regular thing!" Alè shot back.

"Don't tempt me, brother."

Alè began to laugh hysterically. His deep laugh provided me with heart-warming relief. He laughed so hard he began to wrap his arms around Maria and Sawyer, who had been seated on either side of him. As I glanced over to the faces of the others surrounding the table, they all appeared to be staring down while digging their top teeth into their lips to prevent a laugh from exiting their mouths.

I knew they felt safe laughing at Archibald in our presence, but it was not going to come easy, given their years of traumatic suppression. They had to always be on my father's side, no matter how they truly felt, but tonight was different. Alè was King, even if it was just for one night. King Alexander The Spoiled, as titled by my father, was to be retitled tonight as King Alexander The Affectionate. Alè was full of affection, something he only showed to those who deserved it the most, those around this table.

CHAPTER SEVEN

I heard Maria squeegeeing the bathroom mirror across from Alè's room which produced such an irritating sound that my body awoke in pure discomfort. At first, I was a bit disoriented from waking up on the floor of Alè's bedroom, the place I spent the night. I was still not allowing Alè out of my sight, and the nighttime was no exception. The night left six to nine hours of unsupervised time where Alè could potentially put himself in harm's way, and I was not taking any chances given the circumstances. Alè refused to let me sleep in his bed as he claimed I was like "a burning fire log that would make him sweat," but I refused to return to my own bed despite his annoyed demeanour. I laid four large pillows and my duck feather duvet on the hardwood floors beside his bed. I felt a tad creepy as I watched his eyes drift off into the night before I allowed myself to sleep. It was the only way I could ensure he would sleep. If he had to get up in the night, he had to practically step on my body to get by me, an added safety measure of mine.

"Wake up! It's ten in the morning!" I announced while I tapped Alè's shoulder.

"Ughhhhh!"

"Wake up!" I yelled.

"I'm up!" Alè shouted in annoyance.

Alè and I stumbled down the stairs to an empty house yet again. The only other person on the main level was

Sawyer, who had been slicing bacon from his fresh-cut pork belly on the counter.

"Morning, boys!" Sawyer said with a knife in his hand.

"Morning, Mr Butcher!" I said sarcastically.

"HA! Bacon, anyone?" Sawyer smiled.

"Must you slaughter the pig on the counter? I'd rather be oblivious to where my bacon comes from," I said.

Alè didn't laugh at my joke. My light-hearted comment went right through him as if his body was no longer there.

"Alexander, Theo, what can I make for you boys this morning?"

"I'll have scrambled eggs and two slices of toast, please," I politely requested.

"And for you, Alexander?"

"Oh, Uh…I'm not hungry."

"What? Why not?" I asked.

"I'm just not."

"Okay, skinny legend!" I laughed.

Alè didn't laugh at that joke either. He was not acting like his typical self like he'd been shell-shocked or he'd come down with a bad flu. I wasn't sure which one it was, but I knew he was feeling off.

"Still no Lord and Lady Perkins?"

"Afraid not, Theo. I haven't heard from either of them!" Sawyer said with a straight face.

"Hmm, maybe we can have another family dinner tonight!" I replied.

"Maybe!"

Sawyer cracked my eggs and broke them in a bowl before tossing them into a hot stainless steel skillet with butter. I loved the way he prepared scrambled eggs. The buttery pan, in combination with the farm-fresh yolks, created a velvety, silky texture that sent my palette into another dimension. Although scrambled eggs were a standard dish, Sawyer's scrambled eggs were something else entirely.

"Alexander, are you feeling okay, kiddo?" Sawyer asked.

We both turned to my brother, who had a grey complexion. His skin colour appeared to be losing saturation, displaying a hue of a whitish grey. He froze at Sawyer's question as if his brain was processing the file like an old bulky white computer.

"Oh, sorry, yeah, I think I'm just tired," Alè responded after ten seconds of silence.

"You should take a nap, kid. I'll have Maria bring you up a cup of lemon tea."

"Yeah, I agree, Alè. I'll take you back upstairs!"

"I'm nineteen! I can take myself to bed!" Alè snapped.

I didn't want to argue with my brother, so I let him walk upstairs to his room alone. I could practically see him the whole way up, and I wasn't going to be far. I had pulled apart his room while he was in the hospital, searching for every tiny object that could harm him and confiscated them. I had also gone through our medicine cabinet, flushing any pills that were not being used by my family. Alè slowly waddled upstairs to his room and left the door open. I was not allowing him to shut the door behind himself. This house was now a temporary prison. Every private moment was now public until I could trust him once again.

As I sat and ate my breakfast, I scrolled through about two hundred stupid videos on my phone. My phone was like a portal. It could suck me in for an hour, sometimes multiple hours. It was such a toxic habit, but it was so normal amongst people my age. My whole life practically existed on that small seven-inch screen. As I sat at the breakfast nook on my phone, a message from Wes came through.

Wes: *Hey T! Hope ur all good. Can we video chat sometime today? I wanna see ur face :)*

Theo: *Oooh he wants to see my face huh? Well I literally just woke up so my hair is gnarly and my morning breath might spawn through ur phone in 4D so* lemme shower first :)

Wes: *Honestly u dont have to haha. I just woke up too! My morning breath is defo worse than urs :)*

Theo: *Cute. Lmao call me in five.*

Wes: *Yay!*

I grabbed my breakfast dishes and began to walk them over to the kitchen. I attempted to load them into the dishwasher, but Sawyer caught me.

"I will gladly eat with you and break some rules, but if you start doing my chores, that's where I will draw the line in the sand!" Sawyer said.

"Hmm...Shall I go awake King Alexander and request he grant me permission?" I asked sarcastically.

"Let him sleep!"

"Fine!"

As I chatted with Sawyer, my phone began to ring as Wes' face popped up on my lock screen. I excused myself from my conversation with Sawyer and headed to the den for privacy.

"Hey!" Wes shouted.

"Oh my god! I can smell your morning breath from here!" I said with a flirtatious grin.

"Are you sure that's just not the cow manure from rural Milton?"

I started laughing like a child at Wes' Milton jab. My laugh caught the attention of Sawyer as he poked his head around the corner to investigate. Sawyer could tend to be a bit nosy.

"One sec, I gotta walk out back. Sawyer is lurking," I said as I smiled at Sawyer.

I shut the exterior patio door behind me. I was in full privacy in my backyard, something I didn't have inside, with attentive ears all around me.

"So, How is your brother?" Wes asked.

"He's doing better, actually. I had a nice dinner with him yesterday, and he seemed to be in good spirits. He has a fever or something this morning, but overall, he's good!"

"Good, I'm glad!" Wes smiled.

"Me too," I said as a slight tear built up in my eye.

"I can't wait to see you, T. I miss your cute face."

"Hmm…Where is this cute face you speak of? My face is still unwashed and greasy!"

"The shine makes it cuter!" Wes said while repositioning his camera.

"Freaky boy!" I said.

Wes chuckled at me, calling him a freak. Even though his face was only on my screen and not physically in front of me, I could feel his playful energy radiate from his beautiful smile.

"Wes, when things cool down, we should go out to a movie or something. I wanna see you."

"Name a day, and I'll cancel every other plan to see you!" he replied.

"Really? What if Tony DiMattina announced he was doing a meet and greet near your apartment the day I wanted to see you?"

"Oh, Tony can wait!" Wes said with a chuckle.

"That was a trick question. I would already be there, first in line!" I laughed.

"Nope, second. I would pull you by the hair and steal your spot!"

"HA! I'd grab hold of your blond locks and yank YOU into second!"

"Is that so? Prince T is violent! In a cute way tho!" Wes smiled.

"Oh, violence is cute to you? Damn boy, you really ARE freaky!"

I continued to laugh as Wes matched my energy. I loved joking with him. We could cross so many lines, and neither one of us got the slightest bit offended. I didn't have to wear a mask with him. I was truly Theo in his most authentic form. I felt Wes could be himself as well, which brought me immense joy.

"I heard something about you from Jade," Wes smirked.

"Shit! What?"

"A secret!" Wes laughed.

"What secret?" I asked, curious if Wes truly had a dark secret of mine in his possession.

"That you love Dolly Parton."

"Shoot! You got me, Wes!" I sighed as an immense feeling of relief flooded my body.

"Well, I own like three of her vinyls, so I guess I'm a fan too!" Wes said.

"Fuck! Sounds like we're soulmates Wessy!" I laughed.

"I think you're right! What's your ring size? I gotta tell the jeweller!"

"I dunno, but don't get me a diamond! That's too traditional for my taste!" I said with a smirk.

"You think I can afford a diamond on this student budget?" Wes asked as he moved the camera closer to his face.

"Perfect, I'd much prefer an ocean-blue sapphire, similar to the ring of Princess Diana!"

"You think I can afford a sapphire?" Wes repeated as he moved even closer.

"Hmm. Maybe if you stopped buying expensive flat whites from your local shitty coffee bar, you would have enough money to take my hand!" I said.

Wes laughed hysterically at my coffee joke.

"Oh my god! I'm never going to live that down, am I?"

"Not until you redeem yourself with better coffee, Wessy!"

Wes and I continued our banter for two hours. The time flew by like it was running faster than the orange beauty on the highway. I could have spent two more hours on the call with him, but he finally had to go as he had made plans with his friend group and had yet to shower or brush his teeth. I felt a renewed sense of peace after speaking with him. For a moment, my troubles and sorrow dissolved like cotton candy being dropped into a bucket of water. His charming smile and witty voice picked my soul up and gave me a renewed sense of joy in life, something I did not have much of at the moment.

I sat out on the patio for a few hours, trying to soak in every bit of sunshine and summer breeze that I could. The warm, country breeze filled my lungs and put my soul into a state of pure bliss. Every deep exhale cleared a small ounce of stress from my bloodstream.

BANG!

The whole house shook violently. There was a slight metallic click before the explosion went off that radiated across the entire property. The walls vibrated for five seconds while the voices of screaming echoed in the halls of Perkins Palace. I was sent into immediate shock, practically frozen to the patio chair. As the sound rippled through the air, the sonic boom-like wave of violence rattled through the trees. Every bird within a three-kilo-metre radius scattered in a swift and uniform reaction to the noise. Every cardinal that sat in the decrepit maple tree outside of my brother's window practically fell off the branches as they took off for safety. Every tree stood empty and lifeless. I knew that sound was only one thing, having only heard it a few times in my life. I had heard that sound only in the woods, never at Perkins Palace. It was my father's hunting rifle.

My frozen composure faded as I came back to life. I could hear Maria violently screaming as if she had accidentally fallen down the stairs and had broken a hip. She seemed physically intact as I opened the back door. Her panicked glare caught my eyes as she began running up the stairs like a firefighter into a burning building. She appeared to run faster than an Olympic athlete like she had superhuman speed.

Sawyer followed about three paces behind her. The sink in the kitchen was still running, so I knew something must've been wrong if he left his task unattended.

I turned back to the patio door, and David had been letting himself inside, an action he never did. He looked right through me like he was searching for where the rifle sound had come from. He saw that I was intact, so he began to scan beyond me for the issue.

Maria's screaming grew louder, like more of her bones were being shattered at the hands of a medieval torturer.

"MY BOY! MY BOY!" Maria screeched.

I sprinted up each step as my knees began to feel wobbly. I heard a door slam and then the sound of two bodies collapsing to the hardwood floor. I ran towards

Maria as Sawyer had her pinned on the floor, preventing her from moving any further. The door to Alè's room was shut, a sight that made my heart practically stop, from two hundred beats per minute to zero, as the realization finally sunk in. I grabbed hold of Alè's door handle as adrenaline flooded my veins.

"THEO, NO! STEP BACK!" Sawyer shrieked.

Sawyer's voice turned into a shrill hiss, then my brain tuned it out as white noise. He wasn't able to get off of the hallway floor fast enough to physically stop me while I barged through my brother's door. My eyes began at Alè's nightstand, which appeared to be normal. I scanned left to Alè's desk, which also appeared to be normal. My eyes locked directly on the side of Alè's bed frame as they met an image of my brother's still, lifeless feet. My eyes rolled along his legs and past his groin, then up his stomach and to his chest, all of which appeared intact. I followed his chest up onto his shoulders and his shoulders onto his chin. All remained intact. My eyes then met a detonation of dark red splatters of death. Alè was missing half of his head. The other half had been scattered in particles across his bedroom.

I completely lost my ability to hear any sounds as Sawyer's muscular arms wrapped around my torso while pulling me out of my brother's room and into the hallway. My body collapsed on top of his muscular torso, practically using him as a human airbag. His arms tightened their grips as I began to thrash, attempting to break loose from his forceful grip. I felt as if I was wearing full hand and foot shackles in the secret dungeon at the Tower of London. My whole world appeared blurry, like the lens of an unfocused camera.

Maria's soft hand grabbed my head, holding onto my cheek for dear life. Her wailing echoed through the halls of the upper floor like a haunting solo of an opera singer. I glanced up at the ceiling of the hallway, staring directly at the etched pattern on the crown moulding, something I had never seen from this angle before. My vision became unfocused again as everything sunk in. Finally, my world became black as I drifted into a state of nothingness, away from this realm.

CHAPTER EIGHT

The light entered my eyes in a cloudy haze. The loud, obscure voice of Archibald Perkins in the next room bounced off of the walls of the front den where my body was laying. My spine was cushioned on the smokey grey velvet settee, with my head slightly elevated. I could feel there were human legs supporting the back of my skull, but I had yet to regain the optical focus to make out their face. As I slowly regained consciousness, Maria's voice vibrated through her body as we laid together. The lullaby she had sung to my brother in the hospital mumbled from her lips in a soft, traumatized whimper. She sang the lullaby on repeat as she stared out of the front den windows across the Milton countryside. Her stare went beyond the ensemble of Halton Police cruisers and ambulances scattered across our driveway with their flashing red and blue strobe lights. The whole time that she mumbled *Una Mariposita,* she ran her fingers through the part line of my hair, something she always did when I was a little boy. Neither one of us spoke. She just held me while I processed everything in shock.

My father's voice grew increasingly louder as my hearing intensified from my regained sense of awareness. I could now begin to make out full sentences from his demanding, ear-piercing voice.

"I don't give a damn! Nobody will know about this! Am I clear?" my father roared into his phone.

My mother attempted to ask him to keep his voice at a reasonable level as we still had half a dozen police officers and officials in black jackets freely roaming the halls of Perkins Palace. One of them carried around a clipboard and had been drawing out an exact play-by-play of Sawyer's guided story. Sawyer trailed behind the officer while they confirmed every detail of the story, like a scene out of a murder mystery movie. There was no mystery to this murder. Lord Perkins stood in plain sight. All the police had to do was pin his blimp-like body against the wall, throw some handcuffs on him, and bring him straight to Millhaven Penitentiary. I would have gladly helped them if he started a scuffle.

"Leave me alone, Sophie!" my father screamed while my mother bargained for his calmness. "Go make the officers some tea since our maid is too busy cuddling!"

My mother began to back down, taking a few steps toward the kitchen to start up a full kettle. The fact that she obliged and played the part of the obedient house-wife made me want to scream. Whatever Lord Archibald Perkins demanded, he got.

My mother entered the den after pouring cups of hot black tea for the police officers scattered throughout the property. My father saw little issue with my mother serving people as she was not a "true Perkins." My mother was still from a French peasant family in my fathers' eyes. She only lived a lavish life because he allowed it. My mother was lucky, as my father saw it.

"My love, sit up and have some tea," my mother insisted.

"I'm okay, thanks."

"Please love!"

"No," I said in a short tone.

"Maria?" she asked.

"I will have a splash, thank you, Mrs Perkins," Maria said with a face full of sorrow.

My mother poured the English Breakfast tea out of her blue floral bone china pot. The trickling sound that the tea made while filling Maria's cup made me regret my decision to not have a cup. The sight of my mother serving Maria should have been recorded for the history books. This was definitely a first, an extreme rarity.

My mother sat down on the small leather armchair across from the settee that Maria and I had been laying on.

"I love you, Theo," she said.

"I love you," I cried while turning my head to my mother.

"Everything is going to be okay, my love."

"No."

"We will stick together, you and me," my mother said.

"I never see you anymore. Where do you go?" I cried. "Alè and I miss you all the time!"

Maria began to rub my hair again, providing comfort in my confrontation. My mother began to cry as she stirred her tea. I wasn't sure if she had been attempting to deflect my question or if she was truly in pain.

"He's gone, my love, he's gone," my mother whispered.

Both Maria and I began to uncontrollably sob.

"You're never around! I need you. He needed you!"

"I-I-I'm sor—"

"You left every night with Francesco while we had to fend *him* off!" I yelled.

"I love you so much, Theo!"

"Every night Mom! Every night you were gone!" I screamed.

"That is not true!"

Maria began to hold my hand as my heart rate sky-rocketed into panic territory.

"This is not your fault, this is not my fault, this is not your father's fault. Your brother was sick, and he did a selfish thing!" my mother said, wiping her tears.

My father stepped into the den as I internally raged. I wanted the police to take both my parents away, one for the murder and one for abetting.

"This seems like a rather exciting tea time!" My father chuckled.

"Mr Perkins, would you care for a cup?" Maria asked as she shot up from her seat, forcing me to sit up.

"I'm fine," my father barked. "However, now that we are all here—"

"Sawyers not!" I shouted.

"Sawyer, den, now!"

Sawyer popped out of the kitchen and scurried into the den like a scared little child.

"I'm here, Mr Perkins."

"Great, since we are all here, I will be informing you all of how this will play out," my father began to explain while we glared at each other in confusion. "Nobody is to know about the drug overdose. This did not happen. Anyone who does not live inside these four walls will never be informed of Alexander's little junkie problems. Am I clear?"

"What?" I screamed.

"Am I clear?" my father repeated in an assertive screech.

"But, Mr Perkins, the thing is—"

"Enough, Maria! Do your job and nothing more!"

My father's demonic eyes circled around each of us, demanding our silence with their intensity.

"As for the gun incident. Alexander was an avid hunter. He was cleaning the gun case when he accidentally and tragically, I may add, fired a round in error, which unfortunately ended his life. This is the official account which we will tell anybody who does not live in this home," my father informed each of us with another stern glare.

"The official account? Who the hell are we, royals?"

"Enough, Theodore! Do not embarrass me in front of my staff!" my father screamed. "I will also inform David tomorrow in case he heard anything from out in the gardens where he works."

Maria, Sawyer, and my mother all nodded their heads in forced agreement. They held the same energy as a conquered people signing their homeland away to a foreign emperor, defeated and reluctant.

We concluded our group meeting then my father demanded that Maria make him a pot of coffee. As he barked his orders, he never once extruded an ounce of heartbreak. His firstborn's death was just another normal summer day, nothing out of the ordinary.

*

The next day, I awoke in the late afternoon. My whole world had been shaken from the foundation up, sending every level of my life into a pile of debris. Nothing mattered anymore, nothing. I stared at the ceiling above my bed, hyper-fixating on the micro-cracks in the plaster, details I only noticed due to my intense, vacant stare. There was not a single sound coming from the main floor, an indication that Lord and Lady Perkins had disappeared yet again.

I tossed on Alè's cashmere sweater. It still smelled like him. Wearing his sweater was like wearing him on my chest. His bergamot perfume perspired from the fibres, bringing a tear to my eye every time I inhaled.

I walked by his bedroom on my way to the bathroom. The door was blocked with a board, covering only the bottom half of the frame. I didn't want to look too long as the sight gave me intense chills down my entire bony spine.

As I made my way down the stairs, my legs felt heavy, like I'd been given concrete shoes by one of Domenico's goons. I stumbled at a snail's pace into the kitchen.

"Afternoon, Theo," Sawyer announced with a slight mournful undertone.

"Hey."

"Would you like anything for breakf—I guess lunch?" Sawyer asked.

"No."

"You have to eat something," Sawyer commanded.

"No, really, I'm okay."

"Theo, please eat, kiddo."

I smirked at Sawyer and walked over to the front den. I knew I needed to eat, my body ached for food, but my mind was not ready. I sat on the brown leather armchair and picked up a copy of yesterday's newspaper. I was waiting for the newspaper to publish my brother's portrait with some story of pure fabrication of how he died. My father had probably already sent in his draft of the article, ghostwriting for some corrupt reporter to slap their name on. My father had friends within reach to make this happen.

Sawyer entered the den with my breakfast. He had a stubborn, fatherly side. I knew he cared about me deeply, and he just wanted to take care of me, one of his love languages.

"I have prepared for you, Lord Theo, an exquisite array of rye toast, smothered in butter of the Virginia peanut type, finished with a lovely candied blueberry compote," Sawyer said while mocking a royal butler's voice.

"Ugh! You could have at least cut my toast!"

"Right away!" Sawyer announced as he turned for the exit with my plate in hand.

"I was kidding, Chef!"

Sawyer returned a minute later with an espresso, and my toast cut into triangles, the way that my brother liked it.

"I was only joking!" I smiled.

"I know, but I wanted it to be perfect!"

"Everything you make is perfect."

Sawyer began to smile at my compliment, then slowly backed away to give me some space.

I sat and ate the entire plate as I was more hungry than I realized. Alè's breakfast made me feel slightly more alive, allowing my heart to pump a little bit of blood. Smelling his perfume-smothered sweater while eating his favourite toast gave me a sense of his presence. I felt he was with me, despite the fact he was laying on a metal counter, being pumped with formaldehyde. The thought of a bunch of different people touching his naked body while trying to patch up his face with their mortuary cosmetics almost brought my rye toast back up. I shot back the espresso, then tossed the porcelain cup at the dark wood floors below me, turning the cup into a trillion shards of white speckles. Maria came rushing into the room to investigate the shattering sound. I gazed directly into her dark brown motherly eyes. She knew I had tossed the cup on purpose, but she didn't appear the slightest bit annoyed. Instead, she walked over to me, stepping over the ceramic pieces and wrapped her arms around me.

"Breathe. I'm here," Maria whispered.

"I'm sorry, I'll clean it," I whimpered in embarrassment.

"I love you, Theo."

"Love you."

I attempted to sweep up the shards, but Maria refused to let me clean up my mess. Every Perkins mess was always cleaned up at the hands of someone else. We never were responsible.

I spent the rest of the afternoon laying in bed playing Queen's *A Night at the Opera* on my turntable. My body shivered at *Bohemian Rhapsody*, a song that put my feelings into words. I played almost every record in my collection, focusing specifically on the more sombre ones. I laid on my bed, feeling every vibration my speakers made. Nothing made me feel alive like Queen did, nothing.

I began to tear through my closet, searching for something and nothing simultaneously. I stumbled across multiple albums of photographs from my early childhood, each covered in half an inch of dust. My mother categorized each year in its own respective binder, like a historical archive of my life in tangible photos. Some of the books made me smile, seeing photos of Alè as a small child. He appeared very innocent, although his face still looked depressed even then.

He spent many years unhappy. These photographs proved it. Each progressing year displayed a further progressed face of sorrow. I never noticed the progression as it became a slow burn. Spending every day in his presence allowed me to acclimate to it. In an earlier binder, his face looked half-content. You could see a mixture between a kid who was suffering and a kid who was slightly free. There was a photograph of Alè in Rome, Italy, half-smiling while eating a hazelnut gelato and standing next to my mother. They both appeared to be slightly happy but not completely.

In a later and less dusty binder, from a trip we had taken a few years ago, a haunting picture faced me of Alè standing at Peggy's Cove in Nova Scotia. His face displayed a dark, tired complexion. My father's large finger slightly covered the lens, as he was the photographer. I wanted to teleport into the picture and wrap my arms around him. I wish we could use our money to buy a time machine. Maybe then I could have saved him.

Even if I could have used a time machine, Archibald would have still existed. Archibald was always a bully. Going back would not have changed that. On each one of those trips, I can recall my father's bullying tactics.

In Italy, Archibald pretended to leave Alè in an alleyway unattended, a punishment to incite panic in little Alè's mind as he was "acting up," according to my father. He let seven-year-old Alè believe he had been abandoned in a foreign country for a ten-minute period, as my father believed this would teach him a lesson. The only thing the abandonment did was traumatize Alè, something my father denied for years following the trip.

In Nova Scotia, my father pushed Alè "as a joke" onto the black, slippery sea rocks surrounding the Peggy's Cove Lighthouse. Despite the many signs surrounding the area telling tourists to not walk on the black rocks, my father thought it was comical. Alè body slid down the black rocks, scraping his knees and calves on the plunge.

On the way up, he slipped, nearly twisting his ankles as he attempted to climb back to safety. The black rocks surrounding the lighthouse were extremely dangerous. The rough seas can splash up, throwing any person on top of them to their death. The treacherous Atlantic Ocean below swallowed many who dared to walk on the black rocks, something my brother was lucky to escape.

Upset from what they witnessed, a few other tourists called the police on my father, something I wish I had the strength and courage to do my whole life. When the police arrived, my father turned on his boy's club charm, walking away from the whole incident without a single charge. Arch told them, "The boy slipped! I reached out to help him, but he refused my helping hand!"

After conversing for half an hour, the officers left with smiling faces and pockets filled, each possessing two months' salaries. Archibald always won, always.

When dinner time came around, I was not in the mood to go downstairs. Neither my father nor my mother bothered to send me a single text message to inform me of their whereabouts. My phone had a few missed calls from Wes and a few from Jade, but I didn't have the energy to speak to either of them. I wanted to remain a hermit in my sheets, away from the decaying world around me.

Sawyer cooked my favourite food, fried chicken drums and garlic mash, while Maria served me in bed. Maria serving me in my room was a rarity. I never made her do it. The crunchy layer of fried breading that coated the juicy, tender chicken drums paired so well with Sawyer's garlic mashed potatoes. I sucked back the whole plate within a few minutes, my body's way of preventing itself from starving. Maria returned about thirty minutes later to clear my plate. I felt beyond guilty that she was waiting on me, although the rest of the family made her do it daily.

An hour after dinner, Maria gently knocked on my bedroom door.

"Theo, do you have a minute?"

"Mmm. Come in."

"I have something for you, something I should have given you yesterday."

"Huh?"

Maria sat on the foot of my bed while her eyes filled with tears of pain. Her shoulders curved down in defeat like they held the weight of the Perkins family upon them.

"Yest-Yester-Yesterday," Maria mumbled.

I stared at her while her left hand shuffled in her pocket. I could see she was reaching for something like she had lost the key to the front door or misplaced her phone. She sniffled every time she inhaled, which made my heart break even more than it already had.

"We took this from your brother's room before-be-fore-the police came."

Maria pulled out a crumpled page, a page that most definitely came from my brother's journal as I recognized the paper. She handed it to me with trembling hands while her sobs became deeper and more defined.

To Theo,

I left you at the hands of our father. No more could I endure his ways of cruelty. I hope you will forgive me Theo.

Love,
Alè

My arms trembled as I read my brother's poetic note. It was the last piece of him that he left for me, oddly comforting in a sick, twisted way.

"Wha-How-How did you—"

"I should have told you!"

"I'm just glad that you did," I whispered.

My father's role in Alè's death was not a surprise to read. I knew this was the truth. I lived that truth for eighteen years, day in, day out. The line that gutted me was my brother's plea for forgiveness. I don't know if I was ever going to grant him that. My brother's act was unforgivable.

My body filled with immense rage as I sat holding the note in my hand. I contemplated tearing the note into a trillion different pieces, but my hands couldn't bring themselves to commit such an atrocity. I wanted to photocopy the note and staple it to every street pole from Milton to Ottawa, for all of southern Ontario to see. Archibald was the killer. Archibald deserved the public shame.

I wanted to force my father to read the note to face his actions instead of cowardly rewriting the history books for his benefit and image. His image mattered more than anything else in the world.

Some people referred to people as wolves in sheep's clothing. Archibald was a demon in an angel's robe. He sucked the soul out of anyone who crossed him while maintaining a peaceful and bright composure. He could practically kill in plain sight, undetected by those who saw him as a decent man. Alè and I saw through the angelic robes to the beast that hid below. My brother was the only one who dared to reach out and fight the true demon below, making him the primary target of Archibald's choosing. I merely stood by and let the demon work his evil. My brother would never back down, in contrast. My father constantly defended his perfect image, an image he fabricated. There was nothing perfect about the Perkins family, nothing at all.

I tossed the note in my front sweatpants pocket as I threw my body against my bed, violently in a fit of rage. Alè leaving me made me bitter. I hated him for doing it the way he did. He let me find him the way he was, bloody and torn. Archibald should have found him. His hands were already bloody. Therefore, his eyes deserved to be as well. I also blamed myself. I was the one who let my brother out of my sight. I was partly to blame. I hated myself for not being stricter on my zero-privacy rules. My hands were partially bloody like my father's, but nowhere near as bloody, not even a quarter.

I was also angry at Wes. He shouldn't have called me when he did. Also at Maria, she shouldn't have been downstairs doing laundry. Also at Sawyer, he shouldn't have been working so much. Also at David, he shouldn't have been outside. I was angry at everyone. Although I knew none of this was any of their faults, I wanted to blame someone, something, other than just myself. My father was guilty, but I wanted to think we were all his willing accomplices, despite knowing it was not true. I had to come to terms with the fact only one man held the blame, one singular man.

*

Over the next few days, my mother and father treated Perkins Palace like a fancy hotel. They ate some meals, showed their faces every so often, and slept here maybe every other night.

My father prepared for Alè's funeral like he was throwing a grand ball. He seemed almost excited at times like it was his time to show off his lavish taste to his socialite friends. One night he showed up for an hour before taking off to some undisclosed location.

"Theodore, is caviar too much?" my father asked. "I was thinking maybe an oyster bar!"

"I think it's all too much, not what he would have wanted!" I said.

"Oh, that's rubbish! Alè enjoyed the lavish life just as much as you or I!"

"Yeah, but—"

"I should have never asked. I knew you would just be a miserable mess!"

"Sorry for actually having feelings!" I cried.

"Oh, the hell with you!"

I removed myself from the room the moment I felt the tension rise. I had zero energy to fight my father, not now, at least.

CHAPTER NINE

My body woke up, but my mind did not fully. Theo was physically standing there in my room, but I was not present inside the body of him. Today I was going to bury my brother, a nightmare that had incarnated into my reality. Nothing about this seemed real, nothing. I glanced over to my closet. Inside the suit Maria was instructed to have pressed for the event was hanging, stiff as a board. My father chose the family outfits. We all had to wear the same black double-breasted jackets, white wing-collared shirts, ash-grey pleated trousers, and a black silk bow tie. Black tie-spezzato was typically reserved for celebrations, not for funerals. I had always associated a black bow tie with family weddings or socialite events.

All of the Perkins men had to wear the uniform, including my cousins and estranged uncles. The jacket barely fit as my father liked the look of a tight midsection around the multiple buttons of the double-breasted coat. His suit was the only one that had space, as he was too large around the waist to have the buttons tight-fitted. Arch always got to bend the rules, always. I slapped half a container of hair pomade in my hair, looking like a 1920s gentleman in an old black and white Hollywood silent film. I looked absolutely ridiculous.

I knew Alè would have laughed his ass off at my greasy hair, which made me chuckle. My chuckling transformed into tears as I felt a hot cannonball-sized piece of sorrow sink into my flesh and burn its way into my stomach. I wanted to vomit. There was no way in hell I was getting ready for my brother's funeral. I wanted to press fast-forward and skip over this entire day ahead. Instead, I had no choice but to live through it.

"You look lovely, darling," my mother announced as I made my way down the main staircase.

"Mmm."

"A proper gentleman, the strong brother!" my father added.

"Strong?" I repeated. "Alè was stronger!"

"Oh, is that so? Where exactly are we headed to if he was so strong?" my father asked with a sarcastic tone.

"Enough, Arch! Enough!" my mother screamed before I had enough time to respond.

"I will not be silenced by you, woman!" my father yelled.

"SHUT UP! ALL OF YOU! SHUT THE FUCK UP!" I bellowed at the highest tone I could possibly reach before my vocal cords shredded into nothingness.

Both my mother and father were taken back. I never screamed. I was always the calm brother. For the first time in my life, my father looked afraid of me as he stared down my red, inflamed face.

"Theodore, put your shoes on son and get in the limo!" my father demanded while still in shock.

I tied my black leather oxfords and slowly tapped the hard rubber soles along the floor towards the front door.

As I opened the door to the limo, my mother came charging after me in her glossy black high heels.

"I think you owe your father an apology!" my mother demanded as she shut the door behind her, closing us both in the cabin of the limo.

"I think I owe that fat fuck nothing."

"Theodore!"

"What?" I shot back in a snarky tone.

"You were raised a proper gentleman. Act like it!"

"And you were raised a Dubois. Act like it!" I scoffed.

"Theodore! That is enough!" my mother yelled.

"I wish I grew up in France, in your village, away from all of this!"

My mother grabbed my hand as I began to weep. She stopped scolding me, as she could tell I was very distraught. As my mother held me, my father hopped in the limo with a stone-cold face. He looked emotionless like he was neglecting the fact he was burying his oldest son in about two hours.

We pulled into the church parking lot. All of our family and friends had been waiting for us to arrive. I hated the looks on every single one of their faces. They took pity on me like I was some type of kid in the starving children charity commercials. "I'm sorry, Theo!" left every single one of their mouths. It was dreadful. I wanted to rebuttal them with a "Yeah? For what?" and watch them all cower and panic as they had to tell me that my brother was dead.

I hated the sad glances I would catch as I scanned their eyes at the doors, like they were radiating a beam of sorrow towards me. I hated every single aspect of it. When the priest followed the casket in, I had to parade behind him with my father and mother, like a scene out of a funeral of a British Royal.

My father had the family crest draped over the casket like Alè was some prince being buried after dying in battle. Alè would have hated being draped in the Perkins family crest. He never considered himself one. It took everything inside of me not to rip the banner off and pop open the lid to let every single soul in that church see what awful thing Archibald had done. I wanted them to look in and see my brother's half-missing skull where the rifle bullet had torn through. Alè may have pulled the trigger, but Archibald loaded the rifle for nineteen years. Nineteen fucking years.

"Alexander was a man of God! He rests in eternal peace with the Lord, our saviour!" the priest announced when he took the mic.

Bullshit! Bull-fucking-shit!

I wish I had the guts to yell that, but I knew my parents would have had to purchase a double plot for the "strong brother" as well after Arch got his hands on me.

"Alexander led by example. He was a role model to his younger brother Theodore," he proclaimed.

The whole church looked at me and pouted. A few distant cousins began to cry while bringing their cloth tissues to their eyes. My mother and father both stood like statues while the priest gave his god-awful sermon, never once shedding a single tear. The priest sounded like he was reading off of a script. I was waiting for him to call Alè 'Susan' or something, forgetting to change the name from the last copy-paste sermon he gave.

The procession followed my brother's casket out of the church approximately forty minutes after we all packed into the cramped hardwood pews. I began to walk down the aisle, still fighting the urge to yank the banner off, like a magician pulls a tablecloth in some magic show. I wished it was my father laying in that box, that Alè and I were following his casket while pretending to cry like actors in a Hollywood movie. Instead, my father got to walk a free man, and I was legitimately crying. None of it was acting.

"I am so sorry, T," I heard as I looked up to meet Wes' eyes.

"You-you-you came!" I choked.

"Yeah."

"I'm sorry I didn't text yo—"

"Stop! It's okay, T! You don't have to apologize!" Wes said in a comforting tone.

I began to cry once again, but Wes leaned in and held me. It was barely a hug as I stood like a lifeless scarecrow or a mannequin at the mall, stiff and full of sorrow. He held me for a solid thirty to forty seconds until a few people began to stare, my father included. Wes then kissed my forehead, an action I wish he hadn't done, not there, not then. As I looked up, I could see the disgust in my father's eyes. He knew that Wes was not just some friend. It was more than that. He held me like Jack held Rose in James Cameron's movie *The Titanic*. I didn't feel an ounce of shame that my father was radiating my way. I deflected every side glance and ever so slight huff the crowd around me made. I wrapped my arms around Wes and then thanked him for coming. Wes provided the first and only snippet of comfort and happiness I experienced the whole day.

We loaded back into the limo, which had been parked right beside the hearse carrying my brother's casket. As I shut the door, my father waved at a few distant family members like a politician waved at their supporters. He rolled up the black-tinted windows, screening us from his fans. After his fifteen seconds of fame, he directed his attention back to me while I sat curled up next to my mother.

"Theodore, what was that?"

"What?"

"Him!" my father screamed.

"Wesley?" I asked in a stupid, sarcastic tone.

"Did that faggot just kiss you?"

"Excuse me!" I yelled.

"Do not insult my intelligence! Do you take me for a fucking idiot?"

My mother began to whimper at my father's scream- ing. Thank god the limo was tinted. The people outside would have seen how the Perkins family truly operated behind closed doors.

"Are you—Are you—" my father said before I cut him off.

"Gay? Perhaps Lord Perkins, perhaps!"

My father's complexion went whiter than the snow- caps of the Rockies. His complexion appeared paler than my dead brother's. My mother began to hug me to pro- vide a slight moment of comfort in the most brutal com- ing-out moments to have ever taken place.

"Don't you support this bullshit, Sophie! Stand be- hind your husband!" my father demanded.

"I stand with my son!" my mother asserted.

That was the first time in my life my mother ever stood up for me in the face of my father. Where was this version of my mother when Alè needed her? Part of me was proud of her, but part of me resented her for waiting this long. I felt so relieved that my father and mother knew my truth, despite the circumstances surrounding it.

Seeing my brother's body getting rolled into the back of a hearse made me realize everything in life can change in seconds. In a way, him being dead gave me a renewed sense of realization that I too will be dead one day. I realized that I can no longer hide who I am to please anybody, especially not the evil Archibald Perkins.

My father said nothing to my mother or me on the way to the burial. We had to pretend as if none of what just took place inside the limo had happened.

As the doors opened, the royal family had to step out with neutral faces and polite mannerisms to please the crowd of family and friends. I shook the hands of a few of my father's business associates and friends who had agreed to be my brother's pallbearers.

As they hoisted Alè's body out of the hearse, reality struck me once again. The dagger called grief slid its way into my stomach, cutting a clean pathway through all of my vital organs. I could practically taste blood as Alè was laid on top of the gravesite. I looked around at all of the people surrounding my brother. Only about five per cent of them actually cared about him.

Maria tossed the first white rose and then said a Spanish prayer while tears poured down her face. It wasn't time for the roses to be thrown, but I knew Maria wanted to wish her little boy a final farewell. Sawyer looked like he was about to vomit as if he had eaten lobster that had been rotting in the fridge for three months.

As my father gave his self-conceited speech of lies, I scanned the crowd to see Skylar Petipas standing about three rows in. Alè would have been thrilled to know she cared enough to watch his body be lowered into the ground for eternity. I wanted to run up and hug her, but I didn't want to cause a disturbance during my father's 'run for Prime Minister me, me, me' speech.

It was my turn to say the final words before they lowered my brother into the vault. I grabbed the mic at the presidential-looking podium the funeral director had set out upon the lawns of the cemetery. I wiped the tears from my eyes as I cleared my throat. I looked at the speech my father had given me on the limo ride to the church, a politically correct mess of cue cards with generic messages of hope and remembrance. I made the split decision to toss the cards in the front pocket of my jacket, an action that sent my father into a silent rage. His eyes widened as he stood there in disbelief, bracing for my speech of improvisation.

"My dear brother, Alè. I don't know how-how-to—" I began to choke.

"Alè, when I came into this world, I had you. From day one, I had you. These past few days, I've experienced, for the first time, days without you by my side. I wish I could say I was just sad. But sadness does not begin to describe the way that I feel. I haven't been able to put into words the way I have been feeling since you left me, Alè. I don't know if I ever will," I said as I wiped the tears from my eyes. "I don't just feel sad. I'm mad. Although mad doesn't begin to describe the deep anger I feel about you leaving me. In the note you left, you told me to forgive you. I hope one day I have it in me to do so. I'm also mad at myself for not paying closer attention. I wish I had been there the day you tried to overdose. I wish I listened to all the signs you gave me. I wish I had stood up for you more often. I wish I was a better brother to you."

I slowly backed away from the microphone as my father's furious face glared at me with the highest level of hatred I had ever seen from him. I had just exposed Alè's overdose attempt to his crowd of supporters who saw us as the 'perfect family.'

As I shuffled back into the crowd, I watched them all toss their white roses onto my brother's casket. The Scottish bagpipes howled across the haunting field of headstones while we all sobbed. Alè was lowered into the ground, a place he would be forever.

We left my brother behind as we departed the cemetery. I hated knowing that he was stuck inside that lawn of iron gates and granite plaques, a place I too would be one day. I knew that we all would be, but I never would have imagined my brother would have been there before Archibald and Sophie. We were supposed to bury them as old people ourselves, not bury him as a young man. The realization kept making me sick. As the limo pulled out of the cemetery driveway, my father decided to break the silence. I could see he was beyond angry from my rogue speech. His face was a brighter red than molten iron, despite trying to conceal it amongst the funeral attendees.

"Theodore Perkins!" he grunted. "What. Did. You. Do?"

"What Alè deserved, I told the truth."

"The family name is forever tarnished due to your stupidity!"

"Oh, did I hurt your perfect little portrayal of what a family should be?" I pouted in a face of pure mockery.

I didn't know what possessed me to speak against my father so aggressively. The emotions of the day brought out a new side of me, a side full of pettiness and vengeance.

"How dare you!" my father screamed.

"Boys!" my mother chimed in, attempting to play referee.

"Shut up!" my father yelled.

"That's your wife! My mother!"

My father's blood boiled as I attempted to defend my mother's dignity. He shot out of his bench seat and swung his fat, bowling ball-like fist in a direct path for my head. I read his movements before he made them and ducked as his fist collided with the interior window of the limo. I was in pure shock that the glass didn't shatter into a million different pieces while falling to the street below. My mother cowered into a ball as soon as our altercation became physical. Due to the large sound made by my father's swing, the driver lowered the partition to investigate.

"Mr Perkins, is everything alright, sir?" the driver asked.

"Oh yes, see, I hit my knee on the back bench seat, that's all!" My father chuckled.

My mother and I looked at each other, both shaking our heads at my father's lies. Archibald was a master at lying his way out of any situation he got himself in. He could grease the pockets of any person who stood between him and his perfect image. If money didn't work, threats usually sealed the deal. He had an artillery of powerful, dangerous acquaintances ready to make any problem, big or small, disappear from his reality.

We pulled into the parking lot of the hall my father rented for Alè's celebration of life. I had zero energy left inside my social battery. I would much rather lock my-self in my bedroom with my records, my cosy bed, and a fat slice of chocolate cake to drown my sorrows in. Instead, I had to play the role of crown prince. I had to socialize with my father's loyal subjects, a crowd of people consisting of those who could care less about my brother. I cracked open the door while helping my mother step out of the limo, like the gentleman I was raised to act like. I escorted my mother into the hall. My father had trailed a few paces behind us. I was going to attempt to avoid him like the plague at the celebration of life.

As we entered the hall, Alè's large portrait had been resting on a golden tripod stand, an image from his school days. His smiling face made me slightly grin as the photo they had selected was god-awful. I knew Alè would have thrown a fit had he seen the photo on display in a large golden frame. My mother stroked the portrait as if she was caressing her baby boy for the last time. The sight of her touching the portrait gutted me. Maria, Sawyer, and David followed us in as the first guests to arrive. My father did not see them as such. They were still his servants.

"Maria, a coffee would do me well!" My father instructed as Maria entered the front foyer of the hall.

"Maria, do not!" I interjected as I turned to my father. "Get your own damn coffee!"

My father's upper lip started to twitch, a sign of the rage brewing inside his dark mind.

"Fine," my father mumbled.

He knew a screaming match would upset his guests about to arrive any moment. Otherwise, he would have verbally, maybe physically attacked me. The sight of

Lord Archibald Perkins pouring his own coffee provided an immense level of satisfaction, a sight Alè would have been so proud of me for.

As the guests began to pour in, my father had my mother and me standing in a line behind him, greeting each one. I once again heard the notorious "I'm sorry, Theo" leave each of their mouths. I had to bare a slight grin and thank each of them for coming, despite wanting to tell each person to leave.

Domenico Mandracchia and his gang of wise-guy goons entered with phoney grieving faces. Domenico shook my hand with a tight grip. The band of his maple signet ring pressed into the skin of my hand. His ring sat slightly loose like he had robbed it from some corpse, the corpse of one of his enemies. I was tempted to swipe it as a joke, but I much preferred my jaw attached. As they continued down the line, I smiled at each one of his goons, playing the part my father instructed me to play.

After an hour of greeting guests, Jade and Wes entered the front doors. Jade walked right past my father, a man she detested and had not a fibre of fear of. He had mutual feelings for her. They avoided each other in peace. Wes, not knowing what my father thought of him, began to extend his hand towards my father, a gesture that went unacknowledged. After a brief ten-second stare down from my father, Wes took the hint and shuffled down to my mother. My mother practically swatted Wes' hand down as she wrapped her arms around him, an action that was out of protest.

"Pleased to meet you, Mr—"

"Wesley Summers, ma'am."

"Mr Wesley Summers, a handsome devil," my mother said while brushing my hand.

Wes smiled at my mother and then turned to hug me.

"I need to talk to you," I whispered in his ear as we embraced.

Wes pulled back as he smiled at me.

"Of course, T."

Wes was the only thing getting me through this god-awful day.

The celebration of life party commenced as my father called a round of cheers at the podium of the grand ballroom. I didn't see this as a moment to toast anything, but my father had to have some excuse to drink amongst his friends. All guests fifteen and older were handed a glass of slightly-chilled, fine French champagne. I never lifted my champagne. My brother's death was not to be celebrated. The whole room was an elaborate wedding-like ballroom with crystal chandeliers and white tablecloth-covered tables, each with a bouquet of fresh-cut white roses. White roses were selected by my mother, an ode to Alè's character. Had my father chosen the floral arrangements, they would have been filled with black dahlias.

As the speeches concluded, I began to mingle with my fellow socialites. I saw the opportunity to strike up a conversation with Skylar Petipas. She had on a charcoal grey A-line dress, something off a department store rack. Her iconic ponytail was no more. She wore a more mature hairstyle, a shoulder-length side-part that suited her face. Skylar still looked elegant despite not having the wardrobe to compete with the affluent socialites that attended out of respect for my father.

"Hey."

Skylar's head spun around from the bar as she had been ordering herself a short rye and ginger.

"Theo, I am so sorry!" Skylar mumbled like the rest of the people I had spoken to.

I looked at Skylar and gave her a quarter-smile.

"How are you?"

"I'm fine, but how are you?"

"Been better," I smirked.

Skylar felt stupid for asking how I was. Her face showed her instant regret after the words left her mouth.

"I wanted to personally thank you for coming. I know it's not easy being here, especially given how my father has treated you in the past."

"Oh no, it's okay!"

"No, the way my father treated you was never okay!"

Skylar's eyes diverted to the ground as the memories flooded her mind of my father's deplorable behaviour

"I also wanted to tell you something my brother will never be able to. Skylar, he loved you. He always did and always will." I added.

Skylar collapsed into my arms as it was my turn to comfort her. We embraced for about ten seconds then she filled me in on the updates of her life. As our intimate conversation concluded, I made my way over to the table where Jade and Wes had been dining.

"Beautiful speech Theo!" Jade said as she hugged me.

"Thank you, love."

Wes motioned for me to follow him as he stood up from his seat. As we crossed the ballroom floor, my father's head tracked us like a fighter jet. I pulled Wes into a side jacket closet behind the bar.

"Wes, I-I—"

"T, I shouldn't have kissed your forehead. I'm so stupid! Fuck!"

"You're not stupid! Don't say that!"

"Yeah, but—" he began as I cut him off.

"It was sweet," I gushed with a smile. "I'm so glad you're here."

"Your father looked like he wanted my bloody head on a stake displayed outside of your house!"

"He probably does, but I would have his on display before he ever laid a finger on you."

Wes grabbed the back of my neck and pulled me in to kiss me. His kiss began to warm my cold, shattered heart. It was like drinking a hot coffee in the dead of winter while stuck in a blizzard. Every fibre of my body felt alive when he touched me.

A hand, not of Wes', pulled on my left shoulder in a violent, swift tug.

"What the hell are you doing? my father screamed. "And on the day of your brother's funeral. You make me sick!"

I repositioned myself so I was facing the doorway of the coat closet. My father stood as wide as the stone that sealed Jesus inside his tomb.

"I make you sick? You make me sick!"

"Tell your little faggot friend he has to leave!" my father screamed while disregarding Wes' physical presence.

"Fuck off, Archibald! Fuck off!"

My father swung his claw of a fist into the drywall of the closet. It made a baseball-sized hole as he pulled his hand away, covered in drywall dust. I shoved my father aside, giving Wes the opportunity to escape. As I snuck past my father, Wes took off for the doors as I chased him out of the hall.

"Wes!"

"T, I should go! I-I—"

"Wes! I'm so sorry, he's a psycho!"

"I gotta go," Wes whimpered with a voice laced with fear.

Wes practically sprinted towards Jade's car. I knew he couldn't leave as Jade had been his ride to the venue. As I turned around, I realized my father had been watching us speak at the door. Knowing my father, I knew Wes' attendance made his blood boil. He appeared to be fighting the urge to unleash his anger as his face slightly twitched if you studied it closely. His complexion almost appeared calm, like a deranged killer in a violent horror film.

"You will turn around, fix your suit jacket and go back in there to socialize!" my father demanded.

"I'm going to find Jade, and then I'm getting the fuck out of here!"

"You are not!" my father yelled.

"Watch me, Arch. Fucking watch me!"

I stormed into the ballroom, my father trailed half a pace behind me.

"Beautiful ceremony!" Mrs Chang said as I walked past her.

Mrs Chang was an old teacher of my brother's. I had always believed my father and her had slept around.

They were always too close to each other in some sense. I completely disregarded her as my father began to socialize with her.

"Yeah, so beautiful right? A room full of rich fucks WHO COULD CARE LESS ABOUT AL—"

My father's massive fist covered my mouth as I began to scream. I shoved him aside and kept preaching my sermon of truth. Every soul inside the ballroom turned to face the boy who had been causing a scene.

"NOT A SINGLE ONE OF YOU FUCKS EVER CARED ABOUT MY BROTHER. YOU ALL GOSSIPED ABOUT HIM EVERY CHANCE YOU GOT! HE WAS ALWAYS THE MENTALLY ILL FREAK YOU LOVED TO DISCUSS IN YOUR CIRCLES. YOU MADE HIM A MONSTER, BUT THE TRUTH IS, THE ONLY MONSTERS ARE ALL OF YOU RICH ENTITLED ASSH—"

I was tackled by Domenico's goons. My mother and Maria screamed as my bony body smashed into the hardwood floors, producing a violent crashing sound. Domenico and my father airlifted me out of the room by my shoulders while my feet thrashed like an animal being selected to be slaughtered. Jade got up from her seat and sprinted after the parade of goons that were carrying my body away to be sacrificed.

Domenico and his goons pinned me up against the exterior stucco walls of the hall. My custom-fit black suit jacket scraped against the wall causing the delicate fabric to instantly pill.

"You ever disrespect the family again, you will be dealt with, you spoiled little shit!" Domenico blared as he pulled his fist back to smack me.

I said nothing to either Domenico or my father. I was prepared to die. I had just lost my brother and possibly the only boy I ever cared about, thanks to the evil Lord Perkins. My father shook his head in disgust as Domenico cursed me out. Domenico dropped me as soon as Maria and Jade exited the hall. He didn't want to show his 'business side' in the presence of the ladies. Domenico's old-school beliefs on where women belonged and what they could witness may have spared my skull from being bashed in and my face branded with an embossed maple leaf. As Domenico dropped me, my father demanded I leave in his limousine, instructing I was to return home. I swerved around my father as Maria tried to call me back. Not even Maria's sweet, motherly voice could convince me to come home. I sprinted through the parking lot as I saw Wes hiding in the back of Jade's black Volkswagen Golf. I cracked open the door and hid with Wes until Jade made her way to the car. I essentially had become a stowaway at my brother's funeral, not how I intended for this day to unfold.

As Jade left the lot, she called back to us, letting us know it was safe to sit up. Wes and I sat in silence the whole ride back to Jade's house while he ran his fingers through my hair. After each moment of pure chaos, Wes had been there to comfort me each and every time. I laid my head on Wes' chest as his heartbeat grew in velocity while I caressed his blond locks in my left hand. We were at peace, despite the war we had endured.

CHAPTER TEN

The next morning the unfamiliar sight of forest green walls surrounded the lumpy bed I laid in. I panicked for a slight fraction of a second before my brain realized where I was laying. After the disaster that was yesterday, I planned to hide away at Jade's, away from the pernicious Perkins. Jade had given me the guest bedroom, a small dark green room with a singular bed pushed in a corner with a massive laminate desk taking up most of the space adjacent to the bed. This room was more of Jade's study room and less of a guest bedroom, but I felt safe in it.

The room was a stark contrast to what I had at Perkins Palace, a room with my own king-sized bed and walk-in closet. My walk-in closet was slightly larger than the green guest room, something I would keep to myself if Jade's family asked if my arrangements were suitable. The house was an old Edwardian townhouse in the lower city core of Hamilton. My father referred to the area as "dodgy," but I found the neighbourhood quite charming and eccentric on the contrary. Jade spent most of her time here at her mother's house, as her father still resided in Milton.

I walked down the short, carpeted hallway to find Wes, still in his funeral suit, passed out on the couch. I completely forgot he slept at Jade's. The memory only downloaded as I saw him. Wes looked so beautiful, even while he slept. I couldn't say that about most people, myself included. I typically looked like I came off a twelve-hour shift in the pits of a concrete plant, sweaty and dishevelled. His soft blond hair stayed perfectly styled, almost like it had been locked into place by a team of stylists who worked around the clock to keep it neat, like a news anchor crew or actors on a film set. His hand laid across his heart, gently resting in an open fist. He slept like he was standing guard, ready to pop up if someone tried to make a surge to my bedroom. It was just the two of us down here. Jade and her mother slept upstairs. I snuck by Wes as I wanted to let him sleep, knowing he needed it after yesterday.

"Morning Theo!" Jade's mother announced as I stepped into the kitchen.

The kitchen had honey-glazed cabinets and white linoleum tile floors, something common for older townhouses that had been renovated by crooked landlords. The air smelled stuffy, like stale cooking odours from past meals. Most likely due to the fact Jade's mother loved to cook, so the scents were trapped in the walls themselves.

"Good morning Mrs Lambert."

"Oh, Theo, You know you can call me Lisanne!"

"Mom! He's not gonna call you Lisanne. His parents don't want him speaking like that!" Jade added.

"No, it's okay! Lisanne works," I said.

Lisanne's smile radiated warmth and motherly love. Jade was so lucky to have her.

"I'm gonna make some pancakes and sausage. How well do you like your pancakes done?"

"As long as they aren't burnt, I'm not too picky," I smirked.

"Jade bought me this lovely griddle for Christmas. They won't burn on here."

The fact that Lisanne was content with something as simple as a new griddle warmed my heart. My mother was always demanding new strings of pearls or new diamond stud earrings. Nothing was ever enough for her. Lisanne had nothing in my mother's eyes, but to me, Lisanne had it all.

"Mmm, sausage and pancakes sound delish, Lisanne!" Wes said as he placed his hand on my lower back.

"Well, morning to you, Mr Wesley!" Lisanne grinned.

"Does anyone want coffee? I'm gonna throw on a pot," Jade announced.

"Can you make flat whites?" Wes chuckled and then glanced into my eyes.

I laughed at our inside joke, a joke that meant nothing but so much at the same time.

"Afraid not, my espresso machine broke last year, and I never got around to replacing it."

"I'm only teasing Jade. I'd love a cup," Wes said in a comforting tone.

"Me too!" I added.

Lisanne brought a stack of pancakes, almost a dozen high, to the table.

"Oh my god! I forgot to fry the sausage!"

"It's okay! I think we have enough food here!" I said while eyeballing the ridiculously high stack of pancakes.

"No! I'll fry them!"

"Mom! Wes and Theo don't eat much. They're skinny legends!"

Both Wes and I laughed at Jade's light-hearted jab. We knew she meant it in a loving way. No offence was taken as it was one hundred per cent accurate. As I pulled my coffee mug up to my mouth to take a sip, Lisanne began to look at me with sad, mother-like eyes. The kind of stare a mother gives her child who just failed their first math test, a comforting, heavy stare.

"Now that we are all here, with this lovely meal in front of us, I wanted to say from the bottom of my heart how sorry I am, Theo. I know you and your brother were very close, and my soul weeps for you, baby. I'm so glad you have your friends to help you get through this awful tragedy," Lisanne announced while brushing my arm to comfort me.

A slight tear built up in my eyes. Unlike the other lines of "I'm sorry, Theo" I heard from each funeral attendee, Lisanne's condolences actually seemed genuine.

"Thank you, Lisanne, it means a lot. I'm so glad you raised such a lovely girl. I'm proud to call Jade my bestie," I said while looking at Jade.

"Love you, Theo!" Jade smiled.

"Love you!"

Wes began to caress the top of my thigh before extending his hand to mine. We linked hands under the table for a brief five-second period.

We sat and ate our pancakes for forty minutes. Lisanne told nonstop jokes in order to lift the spirits in the room. I could tell she felt my aura of sombre energy fill the small kitchen, and she was determined to disturb it with motherly love. I found myself laughing at each hysterical story she told. The way she recalled family memories was beautiful. When I recalled my family memories, most of them came with a flood of negative energy attached to them. I wished I could look back on my memories and smile, but the Perkins family was not as fortunate as the Lambert family in that regard.

I underestimated how difficult going to sleep was going to be. It was easy being surrounded by a group of lovely people, telling jokes and bantering during the day. As the lights went out, I was completely alone, left with my traumatic memories and sadness. I sat up, staring at the blank green walls like I was staring through them into the void of nothingness. I stared at nothing for hours, sometimes feeling like I was going crazy. Every hour or so, the lifeless image of my brother's shattered skull flooded my mind, sending me into a full-blown panic attack. My largest panic attack awoke Wes around two in the morning. I hadn't realized I had been sniffling so loud, but it was loud enough to grab his attention.

"T, are you alright in there?" Wes whispered as he lightly tapped on my door.

"Yeah, I'm-I'm-I'm fine, Wes," I whimpered through the door.

Wes let himself in. He saw straight through my attempt to dismiss my feelings.

"Move over. I hope this single bed can hold the both of us," Wes said.

I smiled through my tears while sitting up to allow him to join me.

"I-It's just-I-I've been—I am—"

"If it's too hard to say right now, I'm not going anywhere. You can tell me when you're ready," Wes said as he stroked my arm.

"It's just that I can't-can't shake the image," I mumbled as Wes moved his hand into my hair.

"The image?" he repeated.

"I found him! Alè! Well, sort of, but I saw him."

"I-I-I'm sorry you had to see that. Nobody should ever have to see that T," Wes said as he leaned his head into my shoulder. "I'm here for you."

"I know," I cried.

"I wish I could say something that would help. There's nothing I can say that will change the thing you saw, but I am here for you," Wes repeated.

Wes kissed my forehead, sending rays of warmth into my soul like an electric shock.

"I'm so lucky to have you," I mumbled.

"I'm the one who is lucky! A royal prince as a boyfriend. What else could I ask for?"

"Boyfriend?"

"Yeah. You're my boyfriend!" Wes declared.

I continued to smile through the tears, feeling gutted about my brother but filled with life by Wes, all at the same time.

"Do I have a say in this, Wessy?" I smirked.

"Sure, what do you say?"

"Hmm, I do!" I said as I buried my head into Wes' body.

"I do? I don't have your Sapphire Princess Diana ring yet. It's gonna be a while. I'm three hundred missed flat whites away from having the cash."

"We can rob Arch for the cash!" I said.

"There's the boy I know, wild and crazy!" Wes smiled.

I wrapped my arms around Wes, interlocking our necks into one being.

"Thank you," I whispered. "For bringing me up the way you do so effortlessly."

Wes kissed my neck, making me slightly flustered. My neck felt so intimate, like it meant more.

"I-I-I'm not sure if I'm ready yet for sex," I stammered, trying not to offend him

"That's okay!"

"Are you mad?" I asked.

"Mad?" Wes repeated while turning my face gently so that we were looking in each other's eyes.

"Yeah."

"At you? Never," Wes said. "I just wanted to kiss your neck. It smelled fresh."

"Fresh sweat, maybe," I said.

"Even better."

"Freaky boy."

Wes and I sat up all night and just talked. He never tried once to pressure me for sex. He just talked. I felt safe in his arms, something rare for me. His witty banter was just what my shattered heart needed, not pity. I knew he took pity on me, but he spoke to me like he didn't, the most touching part of it all. We talked about his childhood, as mine was too triggering to discuss in a light-hearted conversation. Wes talked about growing up in Ancaster, an affluent town forty minutes from Milton. His mother was a lawyer, and his father was a stay-at-home husband, something my father would never allow. I loved that they played reverse gender roles in the Summers' home. He also told me about the times he travelled all over Europe with his older sister Arianna.

They backpacked through practically all of Europe last summer. He had spent a week in Lisbon, a place he kept mentioning how much I would love. I had been to Europe many times, but never to Lisbon. Every time he would tell a Portugal story, his eyes would light up like a little kid's. I loved seeing him like that. It made my heart beat again.

Wes and I watched the sun come through the small window of the green-painted bedroom. The walls were so dark that the rising sun barely lit up the room. If I closed the blinds, it could be midnight still for all we could tell. Part of me wished that it was, so I could spend another seven hours talking and cuddling.

"Sun is coming up!" I said as I parted Wes' hair with my fingers.

"Do you know what today is?"

"Dunno, what?" I asked.

"The first day where I can officially say I have a boyfriend. I've never had one before."

"A boyfriend?"

"Yeah," Wes whispered.

"Surely, you've had a girlfriend, being bi."

"Nah, you're my first anything," Wes explained.

"You're fucking with me!"

"Nope."

"Well, let it be known all over the kingdom, Wes Summers and Theo—uh Perkins, I guess that's my name, are boyfriends!"

"The royal wedding is gonna be so pretty!" Wes said.

"The king isn't gonna come but fuck him!"

Wes began to chuckle at the cheap jab I took at my father. After my father's recent snubbing at the funeral, Wes was not too fond of him, and rightfully so.

We stumbled up the stairs, still in the leftover pieces of our funeral suits. I had borrowed some of Jade's black track pants as we wore a similar size, and the pants were stretchy enough to suffice. Jade had been flipping through videos on her phone while sipping her morning cup of coffee.

"Morning, guys!"

"Hey!" we both said simultaneously.

Wes and I had made plans to go back to his apartment in the city as there was more room for us there. I didn't want to leave his side, so I knew I had to follow Wes, but I also didn't want Jade to think her bedroom downstairs wasn't comfortable enough for me.

"Um, Jade, I'm gonna go back to my apartment this morning, and T is gonna come with," Wes asserted.

"Oh, that's cool!"

"Yeah, I have a bunch of clothes he can borrow. We are practically the same size, that way, he doesn't have to go home to get anything."

"Did I hear someone is leaving?" Lisanne inquired as she stepped into the kitchen.

"Yeah, Wes and I are headed to the city."

"Okay, love doves! Let me make you guys some breakfast first."

"Mom!" Jade yelled with an embarrassed face.

"It's okay. It's true! We're-we're uhh kind of boyfriends now," I said.

"Oh. My. God! I'm so happy for you both!" Jade said as she wrapped her arms around both Wes and me.

I could tell her intentions were genuine. She was truly content for Wes and me, not once showing a fibre of resentment or jealousy. I had so much love and respect for Jade that she didn't make things even slightly awkward.

"I could just tell. You guys seem so cute together!" Lisanne declared.

"HA! That's cute, actually!" I replied.

"Lisanne, you don't have to go through all of the trouble. We can grab breakfast at the train station," Wes said.

"Train? I'm driving you guys!"

"No! That's so far, Lisanne. I live in Toronto!" Wes said in a shocked tone.

"Mamma Lisanne loves a good road trip. Let's have some pancakes, and then I'll take you guys in my van."

"No, seriously, I can't let you do that!" Wes declared, shocked by her hospitality.

"It's happening. I made up my mind, boys," Lisanne said.

"You're too kind, thank you!" Wes replied.

We sat and ate breakfast, then loaded into Lisanne's minivan. Jade and I sat in the back while Wes rode up front with her. Lisanne let Wes take over as DJ, a mistake on her part as all Wes had downloaded were currently trending pop albums. Whether Lisanne was a fan of pop music or not, she was now.

About halfway to Toronto, Jade grabbed my hand and then whispered in my ear, "I'm so happy for you."

"I know this is probably awkward," I whispered back.

"I had a small crush. You guys seem like you guys are in love."

"I think—I think I might be."

Jade grinned and then hugged me. I was so lucky to have her as my best friend.

The van pulled in front of Wes' building in a slow roll. Lisanne got out to hug both Wes and me before letting us enter the building. Her deep, motherly hug touched my soul in a way I'd never once experienced from my own parents. If my parents hugged Alè or me, it was most likely because someone was watching them, and they wanted to appear close to their children. Their hugs were like hugging a concrete pillar, stiff and cold. When our stiff bodies connected, our souls refused to, a stark contrast to Lisanne's hugs.

Wes opened the door to his tenth-storey apartment, leading me in like a realtor leads a client for the first showing. The unit was spotless like he had the place professionally cleaned. The whole apartment was done with modern industrial finishes, like something out of a magazine for modern designs. Wes had a small love seat in the centre of the main room, made of brown leather with black metal modern-looking legs. The rug was a faux cowhide like he had tried to mix in elements of a country ranch in his three hundred square feet of concrete. Behind the sofa was a queen bed dressed in white hotel-like linens. I hadn't realized his apartment was a studio, but I didn't mind. The kitchenette had metallic stools tucked under the small faux-marble counter, different from the formal dining room I was used to eating at, but I was happy with it.

"So, what—" Wes asked as I cut him off.

"I love it!"

"A bit petit, compared to the palace you call home!"

"Home? HA! Not sure what to call that place anymore!" I laughed.

"Wait, is Prince T homeless then?" Wes said.

"The prince who couch hops, how pathetic!" I said with an embarrassed tone.

"You don't have to sleep on a couch here! The bed is yours."

"You mean ours!"

"Spicy!"

Wes began to choke on the air surrounding him due to his intense belly chuckle. I quickly grabbed his neck to pull his face close to mine. Our lips met as we began to transfer saliva to one another. The temperature inside the small three-hundred-square-foot apartment rose by twenty degrees. It was so hot that I ripped off the dirty, sweaty shirt I was wearing and tossed it into a ball on the kitchen floor. Wes did the same, exposing his skinny, slightly toned torso. My finger glided up and down his chest, making him smile every time I hit his abdomen. He then turned me around to face the array of skyscrapers beyond his glass window wall. I felt his lips meet my shoulders as he caressed my stomach.

"Are you-you sure you wanna do this?" Wes whispered while slowly taking his pants off.

"I'm ready."

Wes and I lasted about ten minutes. I felt so respected and safe in his arms like he truly cared to check in at each step he took. I knew that if at any point I wanted it to stop, he would have without question. I never understood the term 'making love' until what had just happened with Wes. I had hooked up and experimented with a few other guys in the past, but none of them felt remotely the same as Wes. Those other guys used me. Wes saw me as a person. Our souls bonded in his bed, not something that happened on a random hookup with a half-stranger.

We both fell asleep, holding each other's hands. I didn't feel the need to get redressed, I felt comfortable in my fully nude body, and he did in his. We both ended up sleeping for four hours, as the night before was an all-nighter in Jade's guest room. I woke up a few times as sleeping was still a difficult task for my brain to commit to, but each time I did, I saw the most angelic boy in front of my eyes. I couldn't believe that I had actually just done that with Wes. It was pure bliss.

When we woke up, I saw I had a few missed calls from Maria but not a single one from either my mother or father. I could have been hardened in concrete shoes at the bottom of Lake Ontario, but they gave no mind to it. I didn't have the energy to speak to Maria, but I knew I would call her back eventually. I just needed a bit more time in heaven, away from their dramatic nonsense. I walked across the apartment, still unclothed, while Wes watched me with a smile.

"Morning! Nice ass!" Wes announced.

"HA! What a gentleman," I said. "And it's the evening!"

"Wait, what? I'm so confused!"

"Yeah! It's seven at night!"

"Woah! Looks like we should order dinner then, maybe pizza in bed?"

"I'm down for pizza! But make sure you toss on some clothes before you answer the door for the delivery man!"

"Nah," Wes said.

I hopped into the shower, taking the time to wash my dirty, sweaty hair out. I hadn't had a shower in a few days since the funeral, so it felt like I was washing away the bad energy of that day as well. Every slur my father lashed out, every awful "I'm sorry, Theo," washed down the drain. I felt it all dissolve, freeing me of its weight. I spent twenty minutes under the hot water before getting out to dry.

As I threw on some of Wes' clothes, he began taking a long shower as well.

After his shower, he never got changed, staying in his underwear for the night. When the pizza came, I answered the door and handed the man the cash Wes gave me. He refused to let me pay, despite my several attempts to do so. Wes enjoyed taking care of me in a husband kind of way. I had a gut feeling that would one day be a reality, Wes and Theo Summers. That would be my ticket to dump the name Perkins for good.

CHAPTER ELEVEN

Waking up next to Wes was pure bliss to me. I was used to waking up in the chaos of Perkins Palace, so this was a completely different atmosphere. His eyes cracked slightly at the same time his smile did, almost in the same motion.

"Morning, T," Wes said while tossing the covers off of his torso.

"Shit!" I yelled

"What?"

"Your pizza morning breath is rank!" I said.

Wes began to blow his breath in my direction while laughing.

"For better, for worse, in sickness and in health," Wes said.

I grabbed Wes by the back of the neck, kissing him in a swift motion.

"For worse." I smiled.

We laid on our backs, staring at the unfinished industrial concrete ceiling above us. Many apartments had this feature to appear modern, but to me, it looked like the builders had given up.

"We should put some art up there!" I said while pointing up.

"A nice oil portrait of Prince T in his royal uniform!" Wes laughed.

"HA! Nah, I'll hang one of you dressed like the *Académie dite Patrocle*."

"Woah! Slow down. I didn't know you spoke French?"

"Yeah, I'm half. My mother was born there."

"In Québec?" Wes asked with a look of curiosity.

"No, France."

I pulled out my phone to show Wes a picture of the painting by Jacques-Louis David, a French neoclassical painter.

"Dressed? Isn't that guy nude?" Wes asked. "Oh wait, HA!"

"Right across the whole ceiling, wall to wall!" I giggled.

"Spicy!"

My phone began to ring as Maria's face appeared on my lock screen. I ignored the first call, and then it rang again.

"Talk to her! She's probably worried, T," Wes pleaded.

"Ugh."

"Please, she loves you."

"Fine," I mumbled.

"If you need some privacy, step out on the balcony. I'll make us some food."

I closed the balcony door behind me, taking in the view of downtown Toronto. The noise of the street echoed all the way up to the tenth floor, a stark contrast from the country. Hoards of people shuffled down the street, a few in Blue Jays jerseys making their way to the game in the afternoon. The patios were packed with young, vibrant people, all having brunch with designer purses hung around the backs of their chairs. The warm breeze wafted over the skyscraper-lined downtown core, hitting my face and slightly moving my hair. I looked over my shoulder to see Wes inside, cracking a few eggs. The smell of Toronto consisted of Lake Ontario's earthy musk, greasy food, and a slight hint of filth. I loved the smell. It smelled like peace. As I stood admiring the view, I completely forgot I was supposed to call Maria. Before I could call her, Maria's incoming call took over my screen.

"Theo?" Maria asked in a confused tone.

"Hi."

"Oh my god! I have been so worried!" Maria shouted.

"Sorry, I—"

"Where are you?" Maria demanded.

"With a friend, I'm safe," I said.

"Where?"

"My friend's house."

"I will hunt you down, mijo!" Maria barked in annoyance.

"HA! You *wild* woman," I said, mocking a Puerto Rican accent.

"Theo, I need to talk. Do you have a minute?"

"Is—Is everything alright?" I stammered.

"Well—"

"What?"

"It's your mother. She's not home," Maria began to explain.

"What else is new? Did Francesco pick her up in his fancy little black car?"

"Yes, from the hall after the funeral. She never went home afterwards."

"Never?" I asked.

"No, she did come back yesterday after your father left. She popped in for twenty minutes, ransacking her closets and taking five suitcases of clothes and practically every piece of jewellery she owns."

"Oh shit! Did she need to rent a shipping container for all her pearl necklaces?" I laughed.

"Theo this is serious! I don't think she's coming back!"Maria snapped.

"Damn."

"I tried to ask her where she was going, but it was like talking to a ghost. My words went right through her."

"I mean, I don't blame her," I abruptly proclaimed.

"Yes, but—"

"I don't wanna come back either. Arch is crazy!" I cried.

"I know, I understand," Maria cried. "I miss you so much!"

"I miss you too," I replied. "I wish I could come back, but it's not that easy, Maria."

Maria began to sniffle on the other end of the line. I wish I was there to comfort her, but she was in a place too dangerous for me. We spoke for ten minutes, catching up on small talk and local Milton gossip, Maria's favourite hobby. I eventually told her I had to go as I saw Wes plating our breakfast. His radiant smile shot through the glass door, signalling with his eyes that our meal was ready. I told Maria how much I loved her before ending the call and closing the door behind me.

"Are you okay?" Wes asked as I stepped inside.

"Yeah, it's nothing."

"Okay, just know if you ever need to talk, I'm here."

I smiled at Wes while I grabbed my chair.

"Wait!" Wes announced while I stared at him with a puzzled face. "Let me seat you," he said while pulling out my stool and then tucking me in.

"Old school! I like it," I said.

"Oh, also, my coffee machine just broke, so we will have to make a coffee run!"

"Let's go back to that lovely cafe from before!"

"Hard pass!"

After breakfast, we rode the elevator down to the streets below. We were surrounded by hundreds of baseball fans, mostly supporting the Toronto Blue Jays. A few fans passed by, some wearing jerseys for the St. Louis Cardinals. At first, the sight made me smile, reminding me of Alè's comments regarding his bird of choice for reincarnation. I felt his presence with me, like, in some twisted way, he planned for the league schedule to pan out in this way. I knew this was far from reality, but the thought brought me comfort. Wes probably thought I was crazy every time I fixated on every away fan that passed us in the streets.

"You watch baseball?" I inquired as Wes began to laugh.

"Me?" he screamed. "HA! I'd rather watch the grass grow!"

"Yeah, I'm not much of a fan either."

"I used to go as a kid. My dad would take me," Wes explained. "Although, I think I was just there for the snacks."

"The pretzels at the Rogers Centre do slap!"

"Slap?" Wes asked.

"Yes, grandfather, that's what us youngins say when something tastes good," I said.

"HA! Shush! I'm barely a year older."

"Manther!" I laughed.

"Manther?" Wes repeated. "Oh, man-panther, like a cougar!"

We both started laughing on the corner of Front and Simcoe, a busy intersection with many spectators. Every person around us turned their heads as we repeated the word 'manther' in a fit of laughter. With Wes by my side, not a single side glance made me feel self-conscious. We were the only ones on the whole block. Nobody else mattered, like background characters wandering about in a film.

We made our way into a coffee shop, much nicer than the one from our first date. The real marble tiled walls provided a very pretentious, modern atmosphere. They had enormous espresso machines, practically five feet wide across the concrete countertops. The machines must've cost a fortune as I knew that brand could only be imported from a small town outside of Rome, Italy. The staff all wore white button-ups, not the typical casual aprons and T-shirts in most coffee shops.

"So?"

"It's so nice in here!" I proclaimed.

"Right! I've been researching places for a few days!"

"Researching?" I repeated with doe eyes.

"Yeah."

"Get you a man who researches places for you!" I said as I grabbed Wes' hand.

That was the first time I had initiated any public affection without feeling shameful for doing so. The people of downtown Toronto were completely unfazed by our romance like it was completely natural in their eyes.

The server came over to our table, carrying two glasses of water on her tray.

"I brought you some tap, but if you would prefer, I can bring over some bottled flat or sparkling instead," she explained with a slight smile.

"Tap water will do, thanks," I replied.

"I'll give you guys a second to look at our coffee menu. Let me know if you have any questions."

I glanced down at the menu, a novel of thirty-six different coffee choices. Wes started scanning his and then looked up at me as we met each other's eyes.

"Flat white!" we both announced with a grin.

"They have lavender flat whites! So adventurous!" Wes announced.

"Hmm, maybe too much going on there for me!"

"Yeah."

I grabbed Wes' hand as I thanked him for taking me to such a nice place.

"Wait, your coffee machine is perfectly fine, isn't it?" I probed.

"Maybe," Wes winked. "I wanted to redeem myself!"

"You have pleased the prince with your attempt for redemption. Your life is now spared."

"So kind noble sir! Very kind indeed."

As Wes chuckled, the server came back, and we each ordered our iconic flat whites.

"Oh, and a slice of raspberry cheesecake with two forks, please!" Wes abruptly added with a smile.

The server returned to the table about ten minutes later. On her tray, she had our two flat whites and a massive slice of raspberry cheesecake. The coffees were well presented in a porcelain cup with a gold rim and decals that looked hand painted. The milk microfoam on top looked like it was steamed to the correct temperature and texture. The barista responsible knew exactly what they were doing, and it showed.

"Definitely redeemed yourself, Wes!"

"Only the best for my prince!"

"Wow! So good!" I said as I took my second sip.

"I know!"

Wes and I chatted for an hour, an hour that felt like seconds, as we lost complete track of time, staring into each other's eyes. I once again felt we were the only two people in the coffee shop, blending all of the strangers around us into the setting.

"So, I was thinking, if you're up to it, no pressure!" Wes began to explain. "Tonight, there's going to be a country-themed karaoke night at the—"

"Yes!" I cut in.

"How did I know?" Wes gushed. "I figured since things have been hard these past couple of weeks, it could get your mind off of things for a bit."

"I'm a Perkins, unfortunately. It's been more than just a couple of weeks."

"Damn."

The night fell on the Toronto cityscape, a beautiful array of sparkling white lights from streets near and far. The city came alive on summer nights as the youth from neighbouring cities piled into the commuter trains and filled the streets of the downtown core. Wes could navigate the core like a walking map. He knew where practically everything was, quite impressive in my eyes. We had been dressed in some of his floral shirts, as I still had to use his clothes. He sprayed me down with his signature perfume, claiming to mark me as "his territory," bonded by the same scent. The perfume was the exact scent he wore to the comedy show the night that we met. I knew this was not coincidental, but I still found it seductively sweet.

We turned the corner, and there was a country bar, something I didn't expect to see in a city such as Toronto. I was a closet country fan, a secret I hid from many, as most people my age preferred pop or rap. I enjoyed those genres, but classic country had a soft spot in my heart. Alè and I would collect old country and western vinyls, an obsession of ours throughout the years. We would sit admiring the mellow guitar strums, and charming southern accents echo from our speakers. Something about old country made me feel alive, a feeling most other genres couldn't incite within me.

As we entered the first set of doors, I handed my fake Québec ID over to the bouncer. When he questioned the authenticity, I began rambling in the conversational French I knew, the perfect scam. I then caught the glare of Jade sitting at an empty table in the corner of the bar.

"You planned this, didn't you!" I chuckled.

"Maybe."

"Cheeky, my boyfriend is very cheeky," I said with a grin.

"I still get fuzzy feelings when I hear that word." Wes smiled.

"Oh shit! There's Skylar Petipas, Alè's ex-girlfriend!"

"That, I did not plan!" Wes said with a stunned stare.

"Ope, I feel like I should go say hello. Save a seat for me at our booth!"

"No problem."

I walked across the dance floor to Skylar. She had been facing away from the main entrance and didn't see me enter the bar with Wes. I only recognized her due to her distinctive posture and mannerisms, something I saw a lot of when she was dating my brother.

"Hey," I mumbled as I tapped on Skylar's shoulder.

She turned around and scanned my face.

"Oh my god! What are you doing here, Theo?" Skylar asked as she hugged me.

"I know a guy," I said.

"Wha—aren't you still like eighteen?"

"You gonna rat me out?" I smiled.

"Hell no! Who else would I sing some old country bops with?"

"Skylar! Do you want a drink?" yelled a tall boy with light brown hair from the bar.

"Sure, grab one for my friend Theo here as well!"

The boy gave her a thumbs-up and smiled.

"Oh, who's that?" I asked.

"Uh-oh, that's Michael."

"Your friend?"

"Boyfriend, actually," Skylar mumbled as her eyes diverted to the ground. "If this is awkward, we can leave! I completely understand!"

"Oh my god, NO! I'm so happy for you!" I said. "Does he treat you well?"

"Like I'm his queen!" Skylar gushed.

"Then I like him already!"

Skylar hugged me again, thanking me as she pulled back.

"You know, Alè would have been so happy to know you found someone who treats you well. Despite the fact that the relationship ended, he will always love you even if things didn't work out," I said, brushing her arm.

"I know. I will always love your brother, too," Skylar said. "Gone way too soon."

"Yup!" I replied with a slight tear.

Michael walked over carrying three drinks like a professional. He used two cups, one in each had to press the third in between them. I thought for sure the vodka sodas would cover the dance floor, but he proved me wrong, despite my strong doubt.

"Nice to meet you. I'm Michael. Friends call me Big Mikey, either or," Michael announced as he handed me the drink.

"Perkins, Theodore Perkins," I announced. "People call me Theo."

"Well, aren't you a gentleman! Announcing your surname first!"

"HA! Sorry, force of habit! Just call me Theo. I'm not too sure about the other part," I said.

"Wait, Perkins, as in Alexander Perkins' little brother?" Michael inquired with a face of pure shock.

"Yeah."

"I just wanted to say how sorry I am, Theo! I was planning on coming to the funeral with Skylar. I knew how important your brother was to her, and I didn't want her to go alone, but I was stuck at LaGuardia Airport in New York."

"That is so sweet of you, but trust me, you would have rather not been there," I smirked. "Unless you enjoy drama, then it may have been your cup of tea!"

Skylar laughed as she had witnessed the absolute catastrophe that was Alè's celebration of life party.

"Yeah, it got a little heated," Skylar added.

"A little?" I repeated with a grin.

"So, are you here with a group of friends?" Michael asked. "You should join us!"

"Oh, I'm actually here with my best friend, Jade, and my-my-my boyfriend, Wesley!" I said as Skylar's eyes widened.

"Boyfriend? That's—wow! Congrats, Theo!" Skylar said with a surprised stare.

"HA! I haven't told many people, but I feel like you guys are pretty chill!"

"Oh, we won't say anything!" Skylar said as she glanced up at Michael's eyes.

"Yeah, I won't tell anyone!"

"Well, it's not a secret. I'm just not screaming it from the treetops as much as I'd love to!" I explained. "Come over. We have a booth."

Both Skylar and Michael trailed me about two paces behind as we crossed the bar towards Jade and Wes.

"Jade, Wes, this is Skylar and Michael, friends of mine."

Jade looked at me in slight confusion as she knew who Skylar was.

"Hey!" Wes smiled.

"Nice to meet you guys!" Michael added.

Jade began to warm up to the idea of spending the night with Skylar and Michael. At first, she was a bit reluctant, but she became friendly as the night progressed. I kept handing Michael wads of cash to buy the table rounds of shots. I didn't know what came over me, but tonight was a night I was going to get drunk.

We first started with shots of cheap tequila, going down like antifreeze as we shot them back. Next, we did a round of vodka, then we graduated to horrific American brandy. It tasted like sugar and perfume, nothing like the smooth French vintage brandy my father poured for guests at Perkins Palace. We all had quite a few shots, then decided to put our names down on the set list for karaoke. Wes went up first, blessing the bar with his scratchy, drunk rendition of an old country song used in some of his favourite Western movies. I didn't recognize the song as it vaguely reminded me of the Western films I had watched years ago. I knew why he had selected this song, as there were a few repeated lines in the entire thing. Reading the lyrics projected on a TV screen was difficult after multiple shots.

"You killed it, baby!" I shouted as he concluded his song.

Jade looked stunned as I drunkenly called Wes "baby" in public.

Next was Michael's turn. He sang a double-set list of two unknown country songs. He was so loaded that nobody could make out what songs he sang. Despite that, we all cheered him on like his biggest fans. I was surprised we didn't get tossed onto the streets for causing a disturbance.

As Michael came down from the stage, he tossed the mic to me.

"Jade, my bestie! Come with!"

"No way!" Jade said.

"Come!"

"Jade! Jade! Jade! Jade!" the boys chanted while smacking their fists on the booth bench.

"Fine!" Jade replied as the whole section of our restaurant cheered her name.

We both took our sides of the stage, making a dramatic entrance to the solo mic I had placed back on the stand. Jade had selected a duet that I never heard of in my life. I sang the female parts while she sang the male parts, an idea that had the whole crowd hysterical. We had the whole place erupting and cheering like two newly discovered stars. I was able to fool the entire crowd that I knew the song well, but I was making the melody up as I went. After the song concluded, the whole crowd cheered for an encore, something Jade did not want to take part in. Her eyes said what her voice could not.

"Sorry, guys! See you next week!" I yelled as the crowd chanted and clapped.

A few minutes later, a server arrived at our table with a round of whiskey shots on a black serving tray.

"This one's on the house for all of you guys. You guys killed it!" the server said as she handed a shot to each person.

"Thanks! I can give you my autograph!" I said.

"Enjoy, guys!"

"Wait, Theo, how did you even get in here?" Skylar whispered as we picked up the shots.

"Je suis Québécois," I said, pulling out my Québec fake.

"Cheers to Jean-Paul!" Skylar called as she read my fake alias.

The shot went down like acid. This was definitely my limit in terms of how many I could stomach. After twenty minutes of chatting, we hugged Skylar and Michael goodbye, then Jade, Wes, and I exited the bar onto the street.

"Holy shit! What a fantastic night!" Wes said.

"Fuck! I missed the last train home!" Jade announced as she realized the time.

"HA! Let's all crash at mine!"

"Sleepover!" I smiled while hugging the two of them.

We walked back to Wes' apartment. The apartment only had a queen-sized bed and one couch, a bit tight for three people, but we were going to make it suffice for just the night.

As the door opened, the smell of old pizza hit us all in the face.

"FUCK! I forgot to take out the trash!" Wes announced while pinching his nose.

The smell was slightly rancid but not enough to make anyone sick. As I turned around, Jade was holding in her vomit.

"Is it the pizza?" I asked.

Jade shook her head as her eyes displayed it was the excessive alcohol, not the smell of stale pizza. Jade then pushed past both Wes and me and profusely vomited inside Wes' toilet. I was so glad she made it to the bathroom and didn't spray the main room, as the smell would have sent us into a vomiting frenzy. I held Jade's hair back while she vomited as Wes grabbed her a glass of water. Taking care of her was like the icing on top of the cake of a great night.

"Still worth it!" Jade laughed as she pulled her face out of the toilet.

Both Wes and I became hysterical at her comment, practically waking his neighbours with our rambunctious energy.

I walked Jade over to the bed, setting a garbage bin beside her in case that last shot tried to return. Wes boiled her some ginger tea, something to settle her upset stomach.

After about an hour of our nursing, Jade drifted off into a deep sleep. Wes refused to go to bed as he was worried she could choke on her vomit had we left her unsupervised. We decided to pull an all-nighter and just talk on the couch only ten feet in front of Jade. We wanted to keep a close eye on her in case she began to get sick once again. Wes made us a pot of coffee, something to keep us awake in the late hours of the night.

"Wow, would you look at that! The coffee machine repair man must have come when we were out today!" I said.

"He sure works quick!" Wes smiled.

"You're so cute. I can't believe that's how you set up another date."

"The man has got rizz. What can I say?"

"Rizz?" I repeated.

"That's what us Toronto people say for people having game."

"Game?" I asked.

"You know, good at dating and stuff," Wes explained.

"HA! You do have rizz, Wessy."

Wes smiled and then grabbed my hand.

"I'm so happy you have been smiling lately. It warms my heart."

"It's you that has that effect on me. Without you, I'd be curled in a ball, balling my eyes out in a secret room of Perkins Palace, hiding from my father."

"Has he reached out?" Wes asked with a sad stare.

"Not once."

"And your mother?"

"Crickets."

"I'm sorry, that's horrible!" Wes blurted.

"They can both be horrible people. I need this time away from them."

"You can stay here as long as you would like. If you moved in, I wouldn't be opposed," Wes said.

I caressed his arm, sending a shockwave through Wes' body.

"Thank you, I promise I won't stay here too long," I said.

"Nah, the longer you stay, the better!"

"Fine, the moving truck comes tomorrow with all my shit. There's a lot of it too!"

Wes chuckled at my moving truck joke. We continued talking until the sun rose over downtown Toronto. Seeing the sun poke over the horizon and then glare across the row of glass skyscrapers was an extravagant sight. Wes was so fortunate to live here, safe and with a beautiful view to boot.

CHAPTER TWELVE

After we ensured Jade was safe, Wes and I headed out to the balcony to take in the city's views of the beautiful morning sun.

"Do you ever get sick of this?" I asked.

"Never."

"I wouldn't either. Toronto is something else!"

"Well, it has its downsides."

"Mmm, like what?"

"It's far from Milton," Wes gushed.

"See, I view that as a selling feature!"

"But then it's harder to see that beautiful smile and cute butt," Wes said.

"Damn boy, you have me flustered over here!" I laughed.

"Did that turn you on?"

"Kinda."

Wes jumped on top of my patio chair, laying directly on top of me.

"WES! Jade could wake up and see you," I shouted, then quickly corrected my volume.

"Manthers can't be tamed, baby."

"Ew, never say that again!"

We both started scream-laughing as Wes fell off of the chair and onto the concrete patio floor. As we cackled, the sound awoke Jade, who had been sleeping like a peaceful baby.

Jade threw on one of Wes' hoodies from his closet, the communal clothing supply at this point, and then made her way to the balcony. As she stepped out, we recalled the events of last night, laughing and telling jokes about the evening. She thanked us for not letting her choke on her own vomit, but we knew she would have done the same for either of us. The mutual love we had for each other was beautiful, something I had never experienced until I met the both of them.

*

Maria called me seven times later in the morning, all of which I ignored. On the eighth call, I finally decided to answer, anxious due to the volume of calls.

"Theo!" Maria shouted.

"Yes?"

"Please listen to me. Have you looked at the news?"

"No? What's going on Maria?" I demanded.

"Stay off your phone. I will—"

"What's going on?"

"Theo! Where are you, love?"

"What's going on?" I barked.

"I need to see you in person. Please do not look at your phone. I will come pick you up. Just please, tell me where you are!" Maria scolded.

"I-I-I'm in Toronto!"

"Toronto?"

"Yes," I replied. "Staying with—"

"Doesn't matter, text me the address. I'm coming now!"

I turned to Wes to confirm the address of his apartment. He wrote it down on a sticky note then I repeated it to Maria on the phone. Jade began to stare, sensing something was disastrously wrong.

"Maria, what's happening?"

"Sit tight. My phone says I will be there within the hour!"

"Maria!"

"See you soon, mijo!"

Maria hung up the phone. I began to hyperventilate before spiralling into a complete panic attack. Both Jade and Wes tackled me onto the bed as I choked on the dense air surrounding me.

"Wha-Wha—did she say?" Wes asked with widened eyes.

"Noth-nothing, but it-it sounded really bad, like her tone!"

"It's probably nothing to worry about. Probably Maria being dramatic," Jade added to provide momentary comfort.

"I-I-I dunno, guys," I stammered.

Wes wrapped his arms around me, causing my breathing to slow down. I nearly fainted as all the possibilities of what could be wrong flooded my anxious mind. It wasn't fair for Maria to dangle a snippet of information and then demand my location while telling me she couldn't reach me for an hour. I laid on Wes' bed, internally screaming. Wes laid beside me while Jade made a pot of coffee. I was too anxious to drink caffeine, so I declined the cup she tried to pour me.

Jade had been standing in the kitchen, scrolling through her social media feed as she abruptly squealed the most alarming, ear-piercing sound while her coffee mug fell from her shaking hand, crashing to the floor below. She had been on her phone, as I never passed Maria's warning on to her or Wes.

"What!" Wes screamed as he shot out of bed.

Jade had been holding her stomach, looking like she was going to vomit yet again. Her skin went red, then blue, then pale within a five-second period.

Wes grabbed Jade and held her up while her trembling hand passed him the phone.

"Jesus!" Wes cried, unable to conceal his emotions in my presence.

"Please! What is it?" I screamed.

"T-The-Theo, stay there. Please stay there!" Wes instructed.

I completely ignored his demands, charging in his direction in a swift, aggressive motion.

"No! No! Theo, please!" Wes yelled, trying to prevent me from grabbing Jade's phone.

I ripped it from his hands as Jade and Wes began to cry simultaneously. As I glared down, the most disturbing headline sucker punched me in the jaw, practically sending me to the wood floors of Wes' studio apartment.

SOCIALITE SOPHIE PERKINS FOUND DEAD THIS MORNING IN CAR BLAZE

Police and fire crews were called to the intersection of Appleby Line and Campbellville Road to a single-vehicle collision at the intersection around 2 A.M. The vehicle, described as a black four-door sedan, was found approximately ten metres from the road, set ablaze. It is unsure whether foul play is suspected in the crash at this time following a statement from the office of the Milton Fire Chief Richard Dodge and Chief of Police Jacob Farruggia. Chief Farruggia declined to make any further comments until the investigation is complete.

The crash victims have been identified as 46-year-old Sophie Perkins, a well-known figure in Milton and the Greater Toronto Area, and 49-year-old Francesco Garibaldi. Both families have been notified of the incident prior to the release of this information. More details to follow as this is an active story.

My knees gave out as I collapsed. Wes dove down to catch me so that my head didn't collide violently with the floor. I was so shocked and mentally numb that I didn't cry. My human array of emotions was frozen, unable to function properly. I stared up at the bare concrete ceilings as Wes held me. Jade began to uncontrollably sob on the couch, something I was unable to do. Wes' hands stroked my hair while he leaned his head into my shoulder.

"I'm here," he whispered.

After a minute of nothingness, my hyperventilation set in again. My face tingled like shards of glass had scraped against my bare skin as a few tears poured out of my face.

"No! Wha-how-but—"

"Breathe, I'm here,"

"No, but-I was—She's not—"

Wes began to kiss my face as I rambled on in shock. Every kiss made my rapid heart slow down by ten per cent, bringing me back to the room I was laying in.

"Come, I'll walk you to the bed. Lay down until Maria comes," Wes guided with tears rolling down his face.

Wes carried me like a small child before placing my lifeless body on his white sheets. He laid down with me until my phone rang from Maria's arrival call. I wanted to stay here with him, not be forced back to see my father at Perkins Palace.

Maria called a second time as we rode the elevator down to the lobby. Both Jade and Wes demanded to come with me, but I knew I had to go with Maria alone. I had no idea what the next few days would look like for me, so joining me was not an option. Wes held me in the elevator, afraid that I might faint, then escorted me to Maria, who had been parked on the street. He kissed me goodbye, not paying mind to the fact Maria could see. Neither of us cared to pretend.

I sat in the passenger side of the car Maria borrowed from the garage. The car was an old beat-up SUV, something my family forgot existed altogether. My mother drove this car back in the day. Nostalgia set in as I circled my head around, staring at the interior. Maria sat in silence. Her mournful glare knew I was already loaded with the information she wanted to tell me herself, as my face had a vacant, dead appearance.

"There's been an acciden—" Maria began as I cut in.

"Wha-how—"

"I don't know how. The police came to the door this morning around four in the morning, asking if I was a resident. I was the only one home who was awake as Sawyer was sleeping, and David went home for the night. I let them in—"

"Who?" I asked.

"The officers!"

"Okay and—"

"They told me to take a seat, so I led them to the front den, where we sat across from each other. They then broke the tragic news," Maria cried.

"What the fuck! Where was Arch?"

"Out."

"At four in the morning?"

"Neither your mother nor father have been home much since the funeral," Maria added.

"I can't believe this!" I grunted in shock.

Maria looked over, then caressed my hand.

"I'm so sorry, mijo."

"Where is she? My mother?" I asked.

Maria froze, unable to answer my question.

"Maria!"

"She's—her body is being autopsied to rule out anything!" Maria said.

"Oh my god, was she murdered?"

"No, Theo! It's standard!" Maria asserted.

"I bet that fuck Arch did it!" I said as I smashed my hand down on the dashboard.

"Theo! You can't make claims like that without knowing!"

"Sorry—I-I'm just—"

"I understand. I love you," Maria whispered as she rubbed my tear-covered cheeks.

"Love you."

The car passed the Milton town line. The sign made my soul shudder, as this was the last place I desired to be. Milton itself was a quaint town, but the Milton I knew it for was anything but. My version of Milton was Perkins Palace, my personal penitentiary.

The iron gates opened as the SUV rolled onto the property. I had been sobbing the entire drive from Toronto to Milton, gutted by my life. Sawyer was waiting on the porch for us to arrive.

"Hi," I mumbled while a tear left my eye.

"Come here!" Sawyer said as he embraced me. "I'm so sorry."

I said nothing back to Sawyer. The shock of being back in the palace gave me instant flashbacks and filled my spirit with negative energy. I stepped inside to find a silent house, my father missing from the picture.

"Wher—"

"He hasn't been home since yesterday. He only visited for a couple hours in a hurry," Sawyer said.

"Why?"

"I wish I had an answer, Theo."

"I need to be alone!" I said as I tossed my shoes at the front foyer walls, a spot still with wet plaster curing from Arch's physical attack on Alè.

I laid down in my bed for four hours, having a sobbing panic attack every ten minutes while tossing items around like an enraged toddler. I grabbed each of my vinyls from the milk carton on my floor, snapping each record in two in a fit of unhinged rage. I only stopped myself when I came to the last record, Alè's parting gift. The record meant too much to me to break it. I looked around to the rubble of a hundred half records, a disastrous scene.

I ran downstairs to the unlocked rifle cage. Alè's rifle still sat perfectly polished. The holster where my father's rifle sat was empty. My father most likely sold it to get rid of the weapon of mass destruction, either that or he hid it. I tossed a case of bullets in my hoodie pocket, then stormed out of the side door in the mudroom.

I took off in the quad my father bought for David to ride around when he was working around the property. The engine roared as I tore up the mud along the palace grounds. I took off for ten minutes, far enough that I was alone. As I parked the quad under a tree, I loaded the rifle, aiming it at the distant trees. I hadn't hunted in years, but holding a rifle was exhilarating.

I shot an entire set of branches off, emptying multiple bullets into the brush. I had zero intention of hitting anything. I just wanted to feel the rifle explode in my hands.

The sound the barrel produced every time a bullet launched from its tip made my heart shudder, reminding me of Alè's demise. I knew Sawyer and Maria heard the gunshots in the distance, but I didn't care. I pondered how easy it would be to just blow my brains out right here, right now, but my heart didn't buy the notion. I knew I didn't have it in me to end my life, but the thought slipped my mind in a fit of temporary insanity.

I emptied every single bullet into the trees, despite shooting being illegal in Milton. The woods of Milton were not considered hunting grounds, but I was not hunting. I was expressing my deep bitterness and rage at the universe's sick plans.

I drove the quad back to the palace, ditching it near the back door. I then tossed the rifle back into its cage, leaving it unlocked.

"What the hell were you doing?" Maria screamed as I exited the mudroom into the main hallway.

"Nothing!"

"You could have killed yourself! Do you know how dangerous guns are?"

"I know."

"Do you?"

"I do."

I collapsed to the ground as my eyes welled in tears. Maria stopped scolding me and rushed to my aid.

"Mijo, come lay down."

"I'm fine!" I yelled.

"No, you're NOT fine!"

Maria guided me to the front room, laying me down on one of the sofas.

"Stay here. I'll make you some tea."

I stared up with a blank stare, processing the foolish thing I had just done. I was lucky nobody called the police on me. Gunshots were not a normal thing to hear in rural, posh Milton.

As Maria entered the room with my tea, my phone began to ring.

"Hello, is this Theodore Perkins?"

"Yes. Who is this?" I asked.

"This is Detective Matthew Johan of the Halton Regional Police."

"Hi, how—where did you get this number?"

"A woman by the name of Maria provided to me saying that you are the son of the deceased, Mrs Sophie Perkins. Is that correct?"

"Yeah, I am," I mumbled as my voice broke.

"Well, firstly, I wanted to offer my sincere condolences for the loss of your mother. I have been working on the case with the lead medical examiner. At this time, I am pleased to announce that foul play was not a factor in the crash. We are still investigating what we now know was a mechanical failure with the engine, but we will provide an in-depth report of the failure once we can determine the exact cause. We have no reason to believe any suspicious activity led to the death of your mother, Sophie."

"Me-Mechanical failure? How does a car randomly explode, Detective…"

"Johan," he added.

"Detective Johan," I repeated as Maria walked out of the room.

"Like I said, the exact part has yet to be determined, but we do know it was a mechanical failure."

"I-I'm just confused."

"I completely understand, Mr Perki—"

"Theo! Don't call me Mr Perkins!"

"My apologies, Theo. I understand this is all fresh and confusing, but rest assured we are doing everything we can to extradite this process, sir. I also wanted to mention we have recovered personal items from the crash scene and will hand them over to your possession at your earliest convenience at the main station."

"I'll be there tomorrow afternoon!" I wailed.

"Very good, see you tomorrow. Have a good night Theo."

"Yeah. Good," I mocked.

I hung up the phone on the detective in a haste, bitter action.

"Maria!" I yelled as she re-entered the room from the kitchen.

"Yes, Theo?"

"You could've warned me about the detective having my number. What was that?"

"Sorry, he made me give it to him. He was the one who was here, Detective Johan."

"I wasn't ready for that. I need a drink!"

"No way!"

"You're not my mom! My mom is gone! I can have a drink if I FUCKING want one!" I screamed.

Maria began to cry as my shouting appeared to upset her.

"I-I-I'm sorry, that was uncalled for! I know how much you love me!" I said with instant regret.

"I do, Theo. I do love you!"

I hugged Maria and then sipped on the lukewarm tea she made me.

"This will do instead. No drinking tonight."

*

Maria and Sawyer went to bed around ten, leaving me up to ponder in my depressing, dark thoughts. The den had a haunting aura like I was sitting in an abandoned building. There was a slight draft coming from a quarter-cracked window as the Milton air wafted across the room. I lit a few candles and sat with my emotions.

The unconscious need to vomit was creeping up on me like I needed to purge all of the bad energy pent-up inside my core. My soul left a trail of darkness that other people recognized when I entered any room. Only a few people in my life could cut through the darkness, people I felt fortunate to have. I knew sitting in the belly of Perkins Palace was only fuelling the darkness, making it stronger with its bad aura of death and traumatic experiences.

In every corner of the house, I saw the vision of Archibald slowly killing Alè. In every corner, I saw a memory of Archibald correcting my mother like a housewife he considered to be his property. That's how Arch saw my mother, an item he possessed, not as his human wife. My mother played the character he wanted her to for their whole marriage. She never once, until the past week or so, rebutted his archaic, demonic ways. I knew within the past few years of her constantly being with Francesco that she desperately wanted out. Had Alè and I never existed, she most definitely would have left decades ago. Arch used my brother and me as an anchor to keep her here, inside the palace walls.

Archibald and Sophie met when Arch was sailing through the Mediterranean years ago in the south of France. My father had travelled across Europe in a yacht belonging to family friends of his. They toured the whole French Riviera, stopping at each town. My mother's village was a short distance from the coast, where my father had been docked with his friends.

The young Archibald Perkins, one hundred pounds lighter and with double the amount of living hair follicles, asked the young Sophie Dubois to dance in the moonlight of the warm, humid air of Cannes. This dance later proved to be Sophie's greatest mistake, one that she paid for until she departed from this world. The impoverished little French girl was captivated by the wealthy British-Canadian boy who promised her a life of Akoya pearl jewellery and a luxury home across the pond in Canada. The riches came with many strings attached, strings that no money on the face of the planet was worth. My mother deserved so much more in life, a loving French husband who worshipped the ground that she laid her dainty feet on. Instead, she was to worship her cold Canadian husband.

Sophie's life was reduced to the title "socialite" by the local papers, but she was so much more. The story enraged me, running it so soon after her death. Thanks to the reporters, I learned through a smartphone and not through the mouths of my own family. Maria had tried to shelter me from the story, but it was practically impossible given the circumstances of everything.

Although my biological mother had died, I still felt like I had a mom. Maria was the only true mother figure in my life in ways my mother could not be. My mother was too busy pleasing my father's demands of what a wife should be, playing the role of his perfect little queen. My mother never took the time to properly raise her own children, following Perkins tradition. My father was raised by his nanny, Nicoletta, an Italian woman from Calabria. He saw it more suitable for Maria to raise us in my mother's place like Nicoletta did for him. I don't believe Sophie had a say in the matter. What Arch wanted, good or evil, he got.

CHAPTER THIRTEEN

The next morning I snuck out of the house before Maria or Sawyer had a chance to wake up. A warm, humid breeze came over the Milton countryside as the faint hum of a cardinal sang its morning song. There was a slight fog cascading over the neighbouring trees and farm fields, creating an eerie summer morning.

I saw that my father had yet to return, so I contemplated taking the orange beauty out for the day, but I knew that if he returned home at any point to find his missing car, another Perkins would be buried. Instead, I opted for the beat-up old SUV Maria used to pick me up from Wes' the day before. A more humble, casual option.

The engine made a slight choking sound as the thirty-year-old parts came to a violent shudder of a start. The battery was half-dead, something I could personally relate to. The interior smelled like old tobacco smoke, something my father melded into the seats in his smoker days. The radio barely worked as it cut in and out of the stations as I clicked along the country roads. I would have preferred to play music from my phone, but the technology required was not present inside.

Sitting inside her old car, I felt like my mother was with me. It had been years since I last rode in this thing with her, but the memories I did have, flooded my mind rapidly. My mother stopped driving this car when she saw a neighbour had bought his wife, a new Range Rover. Jealous, she demanded my father provide her with an even higher-end Range Rover, something he did that very day. In the years following, my father bought her a new luxury car every two years. My father wanted to appear superior to our neighbours, something he valued immensely.

It was so early that I couldn't have gone to the police station yet, a place I was not excited to be visiting. My mind was still numbed into survival mode, focused solely on getting through the hectic chaos. I didn't want to stop and reflect for more than a few moments. When I did stop, that's when the panic attacks set in, something I couldn't bear to deal with alone.

The gates of the cemetery made me shudder as I pulled in. This was the first time I had visited since my brother's disaster of a funeral. The dirt was still freshly turned on Alè's days-old grave. The ground was so unsettled I felt like I could scoop the dirt by hand and unearth my brother. Even if I did such a heinous thing, Alè wasn't down there. Rather a pile of decomposing flesh was.

I laid on top of the freshly-turned soil, my body making an imprint into the mud.

"Alè! You would never believe what I've been through since you left!" I cried while placing my hand down on the loose dirt beside me.

"First of all, fuck you! Now that I got that off my chest, I wanted to tell you how much I need you. I need you every single day. Mom is gone, yes, Mom is gone, FUCKING DEAD! I don't know what to think, Alè. Her car somehow ignited with her and Francesco inside. How does a car just catch on fire? Am I crazy for questioning this? Now, Archibald, that soulless prick is missing. I haven't heard from him in days!" I yelled. "So many people came to your celebration of life, which I must add was pure chaos. Arch swung his fat fist at my head a couple times, but I ducked each time, making him punch inanimate objects. You would have died laughing! Also, Skylar was there, she hugged me, and she seemed very moved by your service. I can't believe Arch took that beautiful soul away from you. What an asshole! Also, I met a really amazing guy. I think I'm in love, Alè! I look at him, and my heart sizzles the way you would describe your Skylar. His name is Wes. He lives in Toronto, and he's a university student, and he's funny and smart and treats me like royalty. I love him. I also may or may not have made love with him, but that will be our little secret!" I said as I put my finger to my mouth, smiling at the clouds.

I laid on my back for another ten minutes, flying through a range of emotions. My giggling and playful energy became sombre within minutes. My sadness transformed into anger, pure anger.

"Why would you do this to me, why?" I sobbed as I kicked my feet, making shoe imprints into the soil.

I began to choke as I held onto Alè's headstone. The fact that he even possessed a headstone made my stomach tie into a hundred knots. Hugging his headstone was the only way I could hug Alè. It was all I had left of him.

I exited the cemetery gates, only this time, I didn't feel as if I was leaving Alè behind. He wasn't there. The sickening feeling in my gut no longer lingered as I looked in the rearview mirror at the iron gates.

I kept driving, making a series of random turns, with a desire to experience the open roads. I blasted old country songs from a half-functioning radio station. A few of the songs were the ones Alè, and I listened to as small children, making me giggle like my brother's spirit had been tampering with the radio waves.

Wes' incoming call startled me. I didn't have a way to answer his call on the centre dash as the beater lacked the modern amenities to do so, forcing me to pull over to the next parking lot.

"Theo, are you—"

"I'm okay," I said with a sniffle.

"No, you're not," Wes rebutted.

"No, really—"

"Theo! It's okay! Where are you right now?"

"Currently at a gas station. I took my mom's old car."

"Are you driving alone?" Wes inquired with a voice of shock.

"Mmm."

"You should be resting!" he asserted. "I don't want you to get hurt."

"I know—but I gotta go down—police want me at—the stuff," I rambled.

"T!" Wes shouted. "Where are you? I'm coming now!"

"What? That's crazy! You don't have a—"

"Text me the address!"

I sent Wes a screenshot of my location as well as the address for safe measures.

"My app says I'll be there in an hour!"

"App?" I inquired. "That's gonna cost a fortune!"

"Don't worry about that!" Wes said. "Stay put! Grab some water and snacks, and I'll be there!"

I sat in the beater and stared out the window for an hour. The country air filled the slightly cracked windows as I had my iconic blank stare. I looked out across the fields of apple orchards surrounding the lone gas station. I wasn't exactly sure where I was. My mind blanked as I tracked down the country roads before.

An hour later, an unfamiliar car pulled up beside mine.

"T!" Wes shouted as he busted out of his ride.

The car drove away as I opened the door to hug Wes.

"I'm so glad you're here," I whimpered.

"I didn't give you the option," We smirked as he kissed my forehead.

Wes hopped in the driver's seat of the beater, making me ride as his passenger in my own mother's car. I explained the whole situation and where I was going in order to collect my mother's belongings. Wes scolded me for trying to go alone, not wanting me to deal with something so grim, so disturbing all by myself. I was always stubborn in that way, hiding my difficult emotions from people, always self-soothing myself. I grew up feeling like a burden if I had to emotionally rely on anyone else, something ingrained in my head since day one of being a Perkins. Having to emotionally rely on Wes made me feel like a burden to him, despite the complete opposite demeanour he gave off. Wes never once made me feel like a problem, treating me like I was allowed to feel things, a concept so foreign to me.

The beater rolled into a parking spot at the main Halton Regional Police station. Detective Johan instructed me to pick up my mother's belongings recovered from

Francesco's crisped car. I suspected most things were going to be burnt in an unrecognizable state, as the fire was reported to be "violent" by some of the news articles. Others reported it as "contained" or "fast," so I didn't know what to believe.

Wes held my hand with a tight, strong grip in case I fainted at any point inside the station. As the glass doors slid open, my stomach dropped, realizing why I had been at the police station. A queue of people was already formed, practically reaching the main door that we came in. The station smelled like hand sanitiser and cheap perfume, an oddly specific smell most likely from the miserable old clerk running the front desk.

As we reached the front of the queue, Wes looked over to me, then squeezed my hand to provide a slight dash of reassurance.

"How can I help?" the clerk asked.

"I'm here for a meeting."

"Name?"

I stared at the clerk, a bulky woman in her sixties wearing a pink blazer and a white button-up shirt. The smell of her perfume was, in fact, the scent that assaulted our noses as we entered earlier.

"Name!" She repeated as I had completely blanked before.

"Oh, uh—Perk-Perkins. Theodore Perkins."

"ID?"

Her demands sounded less like questions and more like orders from an army sergeant.

"Yeah, uh, one sec!" I mumbled, almost handing her my fake.

I handed over my real Ontario G2 permit as she scanned the document with her eyes.

"Lots of names there, Perkins!" the clerk laughed while stopping to read my ID for personal amusement.

"Hey! Can you please just get this going!" Wes replied in my defence.

"Wow, feisty your friend is!"

"Boyfriend, actually," I corrected.

"Boyfriend, whatever," she repeated as she rolled her eyes. "Oh, it says here you are meeting with Detective Johan. I'll call him down!"

"Thanks!" I replied sarcastically as she handed back my ID.

After ten minutes, Detective Johan came down with paperwork in his left hand and a plastic bag in his right.

"Theo, how are you, son?" Johan asked as he placed the bag on the counter.

"Not so good."

"I know, I understand," Johan said.

"Is that her stuff?" I asked as I stared Johan down.

"Yes, and I will release it to you shortly. I just need a few signatures from you," he explained.

I signed the paper, my hand trembling while the pen glided across the boxes.

"Yup, that does it!" Johan announced as he handed over the bag. "Oh, and I wanted to discuss one last thing. If your buddy wanted to stay here, then you could follow me somewhere more private."

"I'm coming with him!" Wes said.

"Are you family of the deceased?"

"Yes, he is," I shot back before Wes could speak.

I looked at Wes, confused, as he began to comfort me once again.

We shut the door to the private room behind us. I wasn't sure if an interrogation was about to take place like I had been the prime suspect, the true reason they called me down to the station.

"Theo, I'm not sure how to put this. You see, after the examination of the bodies, we had almost immediately determined that the cause of death was blunt trauma to the brain for both your mother and Mr Garibaldi. As you know, the vehicle caught fire as a result of the crash. The burns were so severe that both bodies were unfortunately severely charred from the chest down. Their faces were still somewhat intact, leaving us to believe they may have died on impact, then a fire started from the engine bay, igniting them from under the footwell. We also found two wallets in a duffel bag in the back seat. Both your mother's and Mr Garibaldi's identifications were inside, allowing us to rapidly identify both. The vehicle was also registered to Francesco Garibaldi."

"Wha—Why are you telling me this?" I cried.

"I know this is upsetting, but—"

"I don't think this is the right time for this, sir!" Wes butted in.

"I understand this is hard, boys, but I must say one last thing."

I looked at Detective Johan with soft, defeated eyes.

"We have been unable to reach Mr Archibald Perkins, and we need to confirm a funeral director has been selected to collect the remains."

"I-I dunno, I can't reach him either!"

"Okay, well, I understand this is difficult, but please, this needs to be sorted as soon as possible!" Johan added.

"Okay!" I shouted.

"Take my card. Call me as soon as you know the details."

Wes and I stormed out of the room with my mother's belongings and Detective Johan's contact card. The fact that even the police could not reach Archibald didn't sit right with me. I hadn't bothered to contact him, but I knew Maria had tried multiple times since the accident. Part of me wondered if he was dead also, like my manifestations from walking behind Alè's casket became reality.

I pondered the possibility of a hitman hunting the Perkins one by one. If this was true, I was next. I knew that was nothing but anxious, fabricated lies. Nobody had a hit out on us. Alè died because of Arch, and my mother died in a car crash, two unrelated coincidences.

I tossed the bag under my arm, unable to bring myself to open it up and rummage through it. Detective Johan also attempted to give me the emptied duffel bag that survived in the back seat, but I left it for Francesco's family to collect, as I had no right to take his stuff.

I pondered the possible reasons why both of their IDs were found in one bag. I didn't understand why. If just Francesco's ID had been found in the bag, that would have made sense, but why would my mother's? My mind kept circling in an intense carousel of anxious thoughts, unable to do anything else.

Wes drove back to his apartment after I had informed him I could not return back to the palace. If my father did return, he would not even notice the missing beater, a car he hadn't looked at, never mind driven in years. Maria, Sawyer, and David sometimes used it to run small errands, so the sight of it missing from the massive six-car garage would not spark anything in Arch's mind.

As we pulled into the parking garage of his apartment, he dumped the car in a visitor spot, something that was a bit of a stretch but sufficed for now.

Wes helped me back to his apartment as my legs became stiff as a board, unable to carry the weight upon them any longer.

"I'll make you some tea if you wanna sit and relax," Wes said as he put my things down on the kitchen counter.

"Thanks, sounds lovely."

Wes smiled and then started his electric kettle. I sent Maria a text, letting her know I was going to be staying over at my friend's house. She replied within ten seconds, telling me to be safe, then sent a heart. She also informed me father had come home after days of nothing and that he denied ever receiving messages from her. I loved how much Maria cared for me in ways my parents didn't.

An hour later, I also decided to send a text to Arch, attempting to have some sort of contact with him. I sent the message and never received even a single one-worded response. I couldn't help but fantasize that he was now dead after the hitman that was potentially hunting us followed him home and took him out after he spoke with Maria. If so, I was now a very rich man. I knew there was no hitman. It was all just a fantasy. The money was not mine. Not yet.

Wes cooked dinner for me, a pan-seared salmon filet and steamed wild rice. He then cracked open his laptop and put on one of his favourite trashy reality TV shows. It was one of those shows where the paternity of the father is questioned in a screaming match while they read the results of the DNA test. I knew he put the show on to lift the mood as a light-hearted watch. I admit, I did find myself laughing at some of the couples, as it was fairly entertaining to watch. Part of me wondered how easy my life would have been had Sophie Dubois gone on one of these shows years ago and got the results that Archibald Perkins was not my biological father. That would have been the most ideal situation I could dream of. Unfortunately, I knew I was a Perkins. When they were trying for children, my parents may have slightly tolerated one another. Being unfaithful would have never slipped either of their minds. As time progressed, being unfaithful was normal for both of them.

As the night came, Wes fell asleep in my arms. I kissed the top of his blond, wavy hair while his eyes drifted into a peaceful rest. I stroked his upper cheekbones, caressing him into a deeper sleep while I contemplated life. As I stared off into the cityscape of Toronto through the window, my mind began to zone out, but then I quickly remembered the bag was still unopened from the police station. I looked across the apartment to see the ominous bag still lying across the counter. I couldn't bear the sight of it, so I needed to open it.

I shuffled out of bed, careful not to wake my peacefully sleeping boyfriend. I tiptoed across the apartment, careful not to put too much pressure on my feet. I learned how to walk silently as a child, a skill I used to avoid Arch when he was in a fit of rage. Alè possessed this skill as well.

I picked up the plastic bag, carrying it out to the balcony for my inspection. The bag had multiple items loosely moving around within it. As I closed the door behind me with a gentle click, I quickly took a seat on the patio chair.

I paused for a brief second, then pulled my phone flashlight out to shine on the mystery objects. The bag tore easily with a single poke, sending my finger right into it.

As I fished around, I began pulling items out like an archaeologist hunting for artefacts on a job site. The first item was a wallet, a man's wallet that looked in pristine condition. It wasn't at all charred as it had been protected by the duffel bag. The wallet was Francesco's, something I was later going to return to his family.

Next was my mother's small Gucci wallet, also intact. Her ID photo looked distant, the same stare she had during her whole marriage to my father. She had a couple of credit cards and a few hundred dollars cash, nothing too exciting.

A red lipstick was excavated next. The lipstick was melted, now a hardened puddle of red wax-looking goop inside of a charred metal container. I tossed it aside and kept digging.

My mother also had a diamond tennis bracelet inside. The bracelet was covered in a thick layer of soot, as it was most likely on her wrist during the crash. The clasp looked slightly warped, but the bracelet was in decent shape.

The final item was a black ring. The ring looked so caked in soot that it was hard to make out what it was. At first, I thought it was a black metal ring of Francesco's, but the more I picked at it, the more ash and soot flaked off, revealing a yellow-gold lustre. I determined it must've been on the floor, close to the flames, to become encrusted. I aggressively scrubbed the ring as all of the soot came off. The ring was in pristine condition, with the soot not as bonded to its surface as I had originally thought. A little elbow grease revealed its true form. I flipped the ring over to reveal a shiny engraved maple leaf. My heart sank as the maple leaf reflected the glare from my phone flashlight. Inside, the initials D.M. had been engraved in the band. My stomach twisted in violent motion, feeling as if the inner lining was about to rupture. I studied the ring for a brief moment before setting it down as the gold clinked on the small patio tabletop. Suddenly, I became dizzy as my whole world went blacker than soot.

CHAPTER FOURTEEN

The breeze hit the balcony enough to wake me up. I was convinced an hour had passed, but it had been not even two minutes. The ring appeared even shinier than I remembered, taunting me with its presence. I couldn't wrap my mind around the fact that Domenico's ring was found in Francesco's car.

The two items together made no sense, having nothing in common to link them. I already knew what it meant, but I didn't want to believe my conclusions. I knew Domenico was a killer, everybody did, but my mother? Domenico was outcasted by the crime family to which he formerly belonged, and I now fully understood why. No honourable man kills somebody's mother.

Domenico was not honourable, as perceiving him as such would be foolish. Domenico was not organized. He did as he pleased. Domenico was crooked, something his associates, like my father, took advantage of. If you needed something done, no matter how heinous, Domenico Mandracchia was the man. He would kill his own mother if the bribe was large enough. I was sure of it. Every moral compass that a man should possess, Domenico lacked.

His ring was purely a reminder of how sloppy the stupid bastard was. He allowed a shiny metal custom jewellery piece to be left behind at the scene of his crime, even engraved with his first and last initials.

Despite how easy it would be to bring the ring back to Detective Johan, Domenico was not a man you wanted to involve in a criminal case in front of a judge. Publicly quarrelling with that man—with his powerful, dangerous connections—was like singing your own execution warrant. Even if I could prove that Domenico murdered my mother, I would be endangering my own life. The case would backfire either way. If Domenico walked free, I would get into an accident at his hands. If Domenico was convicted, his goons would cause my accident on his behalf.

I started trembling as I placed the ring on my fourth finger. The ring was so large that when I turned my hand upside down, it slid off and bounced onto the concrete of the balcony floor, making a harsh clanking sound.

I placed the ring back into the bag and then stared off into the lights of the night. It was so clear that I could see lights from neighbouring cities in the distance, something my eyes focused on as I zoned out.

Tears started pouring down my face as I came to the grim realization that I was trapped. I had no way of safely holding those accountable for their actions. I came to the conclusion that my father had ordered the killing of my mother. I wasn't stupid. As she attempted to flee with her true love, Francesco, he took swift and violent action to prevent her from doing so. When my father got word that Maria had seen my mother leave forever, my mother's life was over.

My mother could have also texted him that she left, attempting to rub in her new-found freedom. That was also a possibility and motive for Archibald's actions.

Knowing my father, regardless of how he found out, it wasn't about my mother's unfaithfulness, but more about the protection of his image. He would rather be a widow than let his fellow socialites gossip about how his wife of a less-fortunate background had left him in the dirt. His ego was too frail to allow a poor French woman to take down his dynasty, no matter if that poor French woman was his wife and mother to his sons. The titles of wife and mother meant nothing to him.

Sophie Dubois, whether she knew it or not, was used as a ploy to bring the heirs of his fortune into this world. No local woman with half a brain would have selected Archibald back then. He had to use his time yachting abroad to snag a wife so that he could build up his empire. When she was no longer useful to him, he discarded her in the most violent way possible. The coward didn't have the guts to take it upon himself, instead using a sketchy character like Domenico to carry out the sloppy actions on his behalf. The sloppiness was due to the impulsivity of my father's orders, given the short timeline of events. Had they planned this longer, the same mistakes might not have been made.

Most of what I concluded about my mother's death was a theory. A theory fueled by eighteen years of being a first-hand witness to all of the madness. I saw everything. Every spew of rage that left Archibald's mouth, every physical attack he launched on each one of us, and every attempt to silence us when those things happened. I knew he would stop at nothing to protect his name, protect his dynasty.

I contemplated waking Wes to show him the evidence I discovered. I knew waking him wouldn't solve anything now. Especially not at this ungodly hour.

As I sat contemplating the new information, my eyes drifted into a heavy, deep sleep.

Wes was still asleep as the sun hit my face on the balcony chair. I shut the balcony door behind me as I shuffled inside quietly to not disturb him in his blissful state. I never wanted to take away the peace of his aura. How could my father look at his family and want to do the complete opposite of that? When I looked at Wes, I felt a desire to preserve his happiness and protect him from the evil in the world. When my father looked at us, he desired to deprive our happiness and bring evil into our worlds.

Wes' eyes cracked slightly as I placed the half-torn bag onto the kitchen counter.

"You-you opened it?" he asked with a curious stare.

"Yeah, I couldn't look at it anymore."

"I-I-I'm sorry, T, you should've woken me up. I would have been there for you."

"Oh, it was nothing really, just some lipstick and junk from Francesco's car."

"Oh, I see."

"Yeah, probably gonna toss it all later."

Wes had large puppy eyes, radiating his pity my way. I didn't have the guts to tell him what I found, not here, not now. He had already been through so much, and lying to him was the only way to keep him safe. I knew that had I told him, he would have gone to the police and refused to listen to me as I begged for his life. I couldn't risk him being in the direct firing range of Domenico and my father, so I kept my mouth shut. I would do whatever it takes to protect him.

"I wanna take you for brunch, mon chéri."

"Mon chéri? Wow, you're letting that French half shine!" Wes smiled.

"Oui."

"And why does mon chéri want to take me for brunch and not breakfast?"

"Pourquoi?" I smiled. "I have to do something first."

"And what is this thing you must do?" Wes whispered seductively.

I paused, then looked at Wes with a grin. "You."

Wes' face became flustered as he yelled for me to join him in bed. He had already ripped off his shirt before I could even make it over. As I slid into the covers, our morning breath became intertwined. His warm hands caressed my body, melting my shattered soul back to life.

We only lasted two minutes this time, something I blamed on my lack of sleep and anxious hormones flowing through my body.

"Looks like it will be breakfast after all!" Wes said.

"Shush!" I smiled while I guided his head onto his pillow gently with my hand.

"Let's get dressed. I'm starving anyways!"

"Same!"

I washed my face in the bathroom and started changing into a fresh outfit for the day ahead. I had to borrow a pair of Wes' underwear and one of his shirts as I was yet again stranded without clean clothes. I tossed on my same jeans from the day prior. Inside the left pocket was the contact card for Detective Johan. It took everything inside of me not to dial his number and spew the information I was armed with. The legal way was not the safe way. Too risky for me and for Wes. I crumpled the detective's card and tossed it into the bathroom trash bin, severing ties with the department.

We ate breakfast at Wes' favourite diner, a greasy spoon only two blocks from his building. During the whole meal, I kept thinking about the ring. The fact that the proof of my mother's murder was in my possession and I could do nothing made my stomach churn. I picked at my food while Wes ate his entire plate. I refused to let him pay for breakfast as it had been my idea to go out. He put up a bit of a fight, but I wanted to take care of him as much as possible. I didn't want him to think I was going to expect him to pay for every meal, and it was important to me that I paid for some of them, even if I barely touched a thing.

As we left the restaurant, we strolled along the storefronts lining the downtown core. A few stores caught Wes' eyes while he pointed out things he desired. One of the stores was a record store, the place we had conspired to go to on the day that we met. Records were a trigger for me now, as shopping for them reminded me too much of my brother. I also felt an immense level of guilt for destroying our collection in a fit of rage, something I will never restore to the level we had. Wes seemed confused as he knew how much I loved them, but I couldn't bear to go in.

After window shopping, we strolled down to the waterfront, a decent walk from his neighbourhood, but we needed the exercise. Wes showed me the police boat harbour, a dirty man-made inlet with a few police speed boats docked inside of it. The water inside the inlet looked tainted and unfit for human activity due to the years of man-made pollution. There was a slight aroma of rotting fish and garbage, a scent that made me dry heave, sending him into a giggling frenzy every time I did.

"Smells like decay!" I gagged.

"Welcome to the real Toronto, country boy!" Wes laughed.

"Charming."

"I'm not going to lie. I'm still not used to the smell either, despite living here!"

"Makes your morning breath smell like perfume!" I said.

Wes chuckled and then hugged me. I felt at home with him, like neither one of us could offend the other with our alternating banter.

"I don't want to ever leave this city," I abruptly proclaimed.

"Even though it stinks?"

"Stink and all, I love it."

"Then don't. Stay with me."

I looked at Wes to see if he was kidding. His eyes looked stark like he truly meant it.

"HA! Funny!"

"I'm serious, Theo."

"What are you talking about?"

"I want you to stay with me!"

"I'm only eighteen!"

"Your point?"

"My father would cut me off financially! What would I do for work? I still haven't technically finished secondary school!"

"Do it online, I'll buy you a desk, and you can work from home, our home!" Wes smiled.

"That's insane!"

Wes looked defeated as I referred to his plans as insane. I didn't want to completely crush him, but I also wasn't ready to make a life-altering decision on the spot.

"Just think about it, T."

"I-I-I just don't know what to do right now. I would love to stay with you, build a home together, but I'm overwhelmed."

"No, I understand. I'm sorry if I sprung that on you so quickly."

"Do you hate me now?" I asked as my voice cracked slightly.

"Never."

"Never? What if I—"

"Nothing you could do would make me hate you. I hate that you believe that I would ever hate you. You mean so much to me, Theo!"

"I'm sorry."

"Don't apologize!"

"No, but I'm sorry that I called your plans insane!"

"Well, they are insane!" Wes smiled.

As we embraced, I felt at peace even though we had just resolved the conflict. I was so used to conflict ending with a screaming match, not a hug.

"I love you," I mumbled.

Wes' eyes widened like he was caught in the headlights of a semi-truck.

"You—I—Wha—"

"You don't have to say it back," I cut in.

"No, Theo, I love you too!"

"You sure?"

"Hmm."

"Hmm," I repeated.

"Does this answer your question?" Wes whispered as he pulled my face in.

As we kissed, it caught the attention of a few people sitting on a bench nearby. We both lacked a sliver of concern for what the background characters thought of us. The wind blew Wes' hair into my face, something that made him smile as he pulled back. I knew now that he was my forever person, the way Alè described it to be. I regretted bantering with my brother when he described what this feeling was like. Alè knew what he was talking about. This was different.

In the evening, I decided to cook a romantic dinner for two, my way of thanking Wes for his charming hospitality. I had never cooked anything in my life aside from the odd snack, but I was determined. Playing videos on my phone, I followed every step along the way. I was attempting to make Chicken Marsala.

As I plated the chicken, Wes sat at the table while appearing intrigued by my creation.

"I-I-love it." Wes smiled while staring down at the plates.

"Hmm. I wouldn't get too excited," I said.

"I'm sure it will be fantastic!"

"Hmm."

The chicken was medium-rare, an unpleasant sight to be seen. The cool, fleshy core repulsed me. Luckily, neither Wes nor I ate a single bite, avoiding a near salmonella outbreak. He tried to cook the chicken in the oven, but the sight of fleshy chicken on my plate turned me off. Even after the chicken was done, I completely refused to touch it. Wes took about two bites before disposing of his as well. The smell the chicken gave off was rancid, even after being cooked all the way through.

"Pizza?"

"Fuck yes," I replied. "But I'm paying!"

"Good luck," he winked.

*

After dinner, We sat on the balcony discussing our lives. Wes opened up to me about his relationship with his grandfather, a man that was fairly absent while he was growing up. He was a wealthy man in his late seventies. Wes' grandfather lived twenty minutes from his childhood home but only visited once every three or four years when the guilt set in. Whenever Wes would try to reach out, his calls went unanswered. We bonded over the fact we had estranged family members, that our lives were not picture-perfect. I told him about my own grandparents. Archibald's parents were both dead, both dying early in their fifties.

Sophie had one living parent, her mother, but her father died of cancer when I was four. Sophie's mother wanted nothing to do with the Perkins family. She viewed my father as a snake, the man who stole her daughter and brought her across the Atlantic. Reflecting on what Sophie's mother thought of my father, I realized she was right. The ring sitting in a plastic evidence bag not twenty feet away from us proved that. Her subconscious mind knew who Archibald truly was. His charming rich boy charm did not work on her like it did on many.

After an hour of conversing, The urge to blurt out the truth about the ring grew exponentially stronger. I also knew that if I did, I could be condemning him and me. The weight that the ten-gram ring carried was that of the world. Part of me wished I was ignorant of the truth, that I believed the crash was an accident. If they even crashed at all. My mind conspired with the endless ways Domenico carried out my father's orders, haunting me to the core.

As I continued to speak to Wes, my mind was absent from the conversation, focusing on the murder instead. I could tell Wes was beginning to notice my mental absence.

"Theo, you seem spaced," Wes said as he scanned my distant stare.

"Sorry, just a lot on my mind," I replied while snapping back into the conversation.

"Do you wanna talk about it?"

"About?"

"Everything. Well, anything you wanna talk about, no matter what it is. I don't wanna force you, though."

"It's my mom. The crash is fucking with my head."

"That cop was an asshole, telling you all those gruesome details!" he cried as he grabbed my hand.

"Yeah, that's the part that's fucking with me," I mumbled.

I stopped myself from rambling on about the real reason I was so withdrawn. I nearly slipped and spewed out the information about the ring and Domenico, but I kept it in.

"Honestly, we should put in a complaint with the police! He's a dick for making it so theatrical!" Wes said.

"Yeah."

"The nerve! I can be your witness and help you put the complaint in!"

I began to sob, burying my head into Wes' warm, comforting chest.

"I'm so scared," I cried.

"Me too, me too," Wes whispered as he kissed my hair.

I had to stop myself yet again from disclosing the ring information, biting my tongue hard enough to practically draw blood.

Later in the evening, we laid in bed while I once again became lost in my thoughts. The fact that Archibald believed he was off the hook made me sick. He deserved to hang for his crimes in the town square, the medieval way. I wish I had the mental capacity to kill him, as it would be an easy job for me.

Unfortunately, I was a lover, not a killer. I didn't have it in me to hire a hitman like Archibald had. Unlike Arch, I possessed a moral compass. Killing was something I could only do if I had to defend myself or Wes.

As I looked over to Wes, I came to the realization that I could truly kill for him. I would use every last fibre of strength I possessed to fight for his survival, something I wish I had done for Alè.

The guilt of not protecting my brother would forever haunt me. His death made me realize that sometimes physical violence is warranted, something I learned too late. I wished I could time travel and get violent with Archibald every time he attempted to pick on my brother. Although Arch physically overpowered me, maybe had I given him a few left hooks to the face, he would have been reluctant to initiate his bullying ways.

The realization began to set in as I laid beside Wes that the war wasn't going to end until I declared independence from the colony. I knew I had to storm Perkins Palace, ring in hand, and stare down the killer while making it known I was a powerful force. He needed to know I was not going to believe another lie of his ever again. Confronting Arch about what he did would make him respect me, knowing he couldn't pull the wool over my eyes any longer. He needed to understand that I was not just someone he could shake hands with whilst driving a dagger into their exposed backside.

After Wes fell asleep in my arms, I kissed his forehead before writing him my farewell letter. I didn't want to consider it as such, as I fully planned on returning the same day, but I wasn't oblivious to the fact that anything could happen. Should I not make it out alive, I needed him to know how much I loved him whilst not causing his mind to spiral into the worst of possibilities. I knew that had he uncovered my plan, Wes would have attempted to prevent me from going. He needed to stay ignorant. That was the only way I could save his life. One day when we were grey and old, relaxing at our seaside villa in the south of France, I would tell him the truth about Archibald. If I wanted to see that, I had to do this first.

Wessy,

I will be back soon. Something came up with my crazy family that I had to deal with.

Please don't worry, mon chéri.

Love,
T

I set the note down on the kitchen counter and then sat down on the sofa, staring out at the skyline.

When the sun started to peak over the horizon, I snuck out, using my key to lock my precious boy in. He was safe here, the only place I could ensure that he was.

CHAPTER FIFTEEN

My mind was blank as I started the beater in the parking garage. Not a single intelligent thought came into my head until I left the downtown core. The old SUV chugged along the highway, fighting for power as I pressed down the sluggish, unresponsive accelerator. No matter how fast I demanded it to drive, the beater could only move as fast as it wished. The Gardiner Expressway was empty, a rare sight to be seen. With each turn I made, the weight of the situation kept getting heavier.

I needed Archibald to know that I knew his perfect image was purely a fabrication of his sick, disturbed mind. Maybe then he would know the power I held. He would be afraid of me and not the other way around. I needed him to know I was not easily fooled like his ring of supporters was. I knew the real Archibald, the killer Archibald.

The ring supported my theory, a theory that I knew was one thousand per cent true. I knew I had to internally stop referring to it as a theory, as it was not. I was correct and had to stay true to that.

As I passed the Milton town sign, my pupils widened, and my stare became blank. The autopilot function in my brain engaged, steering me in the direction of Perkins Palace.

The tires made a slight screech as I pulled down the long driveway. The larger the palace appeared, the more my stomach knots tightened. I parked the beater in the driveway, facing towards the road, in case I had to make a swift exit. I didn't know what to expect. Things could go very wrong, very fast, and I needed to ensure I had a lifeboat ready to launch on this sinking ship of a dynasty. I wiped the ring one last time in the driveway, buffing it to ensure the markings were indisputable when I needed it. The engraved *D.M.* made me sick. The fact that Domenico Mandracchia had the guts to dine with my mother, with his charming smile and witty banter at this very house, made me physically ill. I tossed the ring in my pocket, waiting for the perfect moment to drop my bombshell.

As the front door creaked open, I could smell Sawyer preparing a feast for Archibald's daily breakfast. The air smelled of fried bacon with the slightly sweet aroma of brown sugar and cinnamon. Archibald loved his cinnamon brown sugar pancakes, his typical breakfast choice. The smell was quite overpowering, practically nauseating.

"Theo!" Sawyer called, dropping his things.

"Hey."

"Whe-Where did—"

"I was busy. I had some things to do."

"Ominous, what things?" Sawyer said.

"Things," I replied in a short tone. "Where's Arch—"

"Sleeping still," Sawyer cut in as he scanned my face in confusion.

I knew he was trying to grasp why I was so short with him. I didn't mean to be rude, but I was at the palace for business, not for small talk and banter.

"Did you want me to cook you something for breakfast?"

"Nope. I'm fine, thanks."

"Okay, kiddo. If you change your mind, I'll gladly fry something up."

"Thanks."

Maria entered the room, practically dropping the broom she had been carrying as she saw me standing in the kitchen.

"Th—what—you're home!"

"Home?" I repeated with a sarcastic face.

"Did you bring your-your-your friend, the blond one?" Maria asked.

"No, not here. I don't want him here."

Maria looked at me with a defeated glare.

"And he's not my friend. He's more than that to me. Wes is my boyfriend, actually."

Sawyer's eyebrows raised as he quickly set down the spatula he had been using to prepare breakfast.

"Wow! That-that's great, Theo! I'm so happy for you, kiddo!" Sawyer said as he gave me a side hug.

I knew Sawyer witnessed the forehead kiss outside of the church, so it was likely he was playing along, trying to comfort my vulnerable declaration.

"I will always love you, mijo," Maria added

"Yeah. I just don't wanna hide it anymore. That's what we are, boyfriends."

"Does your father know?" Sawyer asked with a nervous grin.

"Sort of."

The stairs made a larger set of thuds as Archibald carried his large legs down each wood step. Each step made my anxiety flare in exponential intensity, a feeling strong enough to make my heart jump up fifty beats per minute higher.

"Well, I will be damned! He finally showed up!"

I stared at Archibald with a stern glare, making him slightly cautious of me, almost like he knew I was onto him.

"Well, aren't you gonna greet me? I didn't raise you to stare and ignore your elders!" Archibald demanded.

"Hello."

"That's it? No apology? What, did you run out of cash and you had to make a stop at the bank before leaving again?" Archibald asked.

"I'm not after a single loonie."

"Miss me then?"

I batted my eyelashes, ignoring his question.

"I was going to buy you a real car. Instead, you chose to ride that rusty old junker. How humble of you!" he scoffed. "What? You think I didn't notice?"

"It reminds me of Mom."

"Ah! Yes! This is about your mother! Come here, son. I'm so sorry she's gone," Archibald said while motioning for me to come over and hug him.

I looked at Maria as her glare became just as confused as mine. Archibald almost never hugged me in private, not in many years.

"It's gonna be okay," Archibald announced as he patted my back like someone did for a choking infant.

His private hug felt like his public hugs, a cold concrete pole of a man embracing you with a spiritual blocker up. My soul rejected his while his rejected mine. No intertwining took place, not even the slightest fibre of connection.

"Well! Let's put all of our differences aside and have some breakfast!" Arch demanded.

"I'm not hungry," I replied.

"Well, I am. Sit with me, son."

I sat and watched the piggish Archibald Perkins gorge on enough food for a small family of four. He piled the food down, plate after plate, all while not acknowledging my presence. I stuck my hand in my pocket, fumbling with the ring like a fidget toy. After a few servings, he finally broke the silence.

"So, why are you here?" Arch asked as I watched him suck back his bacon.

"To talk."

"Well, start talking! I'm going to be fairly busy this afternoon, so make it haste!"

"Not sure where to start, actually."

"Well, I am! Let's start with the fact that if you do not kick that little faggot friend of yours to the curb, there will not be a single cent left to you when I go. When the day comes, and I am grey and old, you will be left with nothing!" Archibald screamed as he slammed his fist down.

"I'm not going to take that from you," I asserted.

"Excuse me?"

"Was I not speaking English?" I asked.

"You have some nerve!"

Maria poked her head into the room.

"Maria, not now, woman!"

Maria backed out, seeing that I was physically un-harmed.

"If you think you will come to MY home and speak to ME in the pure disrespect you have for me, I will do something about it!"

I wanted to tell Archibald that I knew exactly what he did to family members who didn't obey, but my ego was not large enough to put my life on the line. I still intended to show him the ring but I needed him in a calmer state so that he didn't reach over the table and shove his syrup-covered fork into my jugular.

"I hope you're not here to get my blessing or something! Because that faggot will never be one of us!"

"I'm gay! What the fuck do you expect me to do?" I screamed.

Arch's palm collided with my left cheek. The weight of his hand nearly knocked me into a coma. I took the smack like the fighter I was.

"You disgust me," he gagged. "With your new lifestyle, the Perkins name will be over! Do you understand that?"

"I do! Better that way!"

Archibald swung again, only this time I ducked, making him over-stretch his arm, nearly knocking his dining chair over. The sight almost made me giggle, hoping he would have plunged to the dining room floor. The weight of his body would have caused the chandelier to fall on top of him from the aftershock trembling through the walls and ceiling.

I ran upstairs, attempting to lock myself in my room until Archibald had a chance to cool down slightly. The room was in pristine condition as Maria had cleaned up the mess of shattered records and smashed debris. Yet again, she cleaned a Perkins' mess.

Arch stormed up about two minutes later, pounding on my bedroom door before letting himself in.

"Are you ready to apologize to me yet?" he blared.

"To you?"

"I will give you the chance to do so!"

"And if I don't, will I end up at the morgue?"

"I beg your pardon!" Archibald screamed with a puzzled face.

I instantly regretted shouting that. I considered my life near its end now that I had brought the topic of my mother's murder to the surface.

"I said what I said."

"I heard you! I just don't understand!"

"Cut the act, Archibald!"

"What did you just call me? I am your father!"

"Unfortunately."

"What is that supposed to mean?"

I pulled the ring from my pocket, trembling in fear and rage. Archibald's innocent mask dropped the second the maple leaf sparkled in his eyes. His face went stone cold as his eyes scanned the realms for an answer to the ring.

"Why do you have Domenico's ring?" he asked with a calm voice trying to appear innocent once again.

"Domenico is a sloppy man."

"I'm not quite sure I understand!" Arch replied.

"Cut the shit!" I asserted.

"What's the matter, Theodore?" He smiled.

"Stop!"

"So you found his ring. I'm sure Zio Dom will be so thrilled to get it back!"

"Do you think I'm stupid?" I asked.

"A nice ring, isn't it? I think it's eighteen-karat gold!"

"The POLICE found this fucking ring!" I shouted.

"No, they didn't find that ring. You found it!"

"What?"

"You found it, Theodore. Now if you would kindly give that back, I can—"

"The police gave it to me!" I repeated.

"If you're a bit confused, that's okay, son. We can sort this out," Arch said with a grin.

"Stop!"

"I think you and I both know you found that ring on the kitchen countertop. You remember that, right?" Archibald smiled. "I think you and I know that ring ended up here because Zio Dom dropped it when he was here for dinner."

"What game is this?"

"Silly kid you are! Zio Dom loves you very much. Please give me the ring now, Theodore."

"No! Fuck off!"

"You don't want to play whatever little game you're trying to—"

"Fucking stop!"

Archibald began to corner me in the corner of my room. His body blocked the light coming from the hallway, pinning me in like an animal in a hunter's trap.

"I'm sure you're smart enough to know even I cannot protect you."

"You never did!"

"Save yourself. This is your ticket out." Archibald grinned. "Ring, now!"

I pushed past Arch, but he was able to extend his arm, sending my stumbling body to the floor. The large thud sent Sawyer sprinting upstairs.

"What the hell is going on, Mr Perkins?" Sawyer screamed, seeing me spread across my bedroom floor.

"I'm not sure this concerns you, Sawyer!" Arch said.

"I think it does, actually!" Sawyer corrected.

"No, it does not!" Archibald yelled.

Archibald began to shake me for the ring, causing Sawyer to rush to my aid. To my surprise, Sawyer began to get physical, shoving Arch off of me with every fibre of strength he possessed. The shove caught Arch off guard, his face stunned in a straight, confused pose. The confusion turned into demonic rage.

Sawyer's face was met by Archibald's fist, sending his body into the walls of my bedroom.

Sawyer quickly bounced up, socking Arch in the face. The punch made a violent clicking sound as it bounced into his face fat. Arch quickly shook the punch off, twitching his neck to show he was ready for more.

Sawyer dodged his violent swing, sending Arch to the ground from his own overpowered motion. The fact that Sawyer outsmarted him made Arch's face inflamed with anger.

As he laid on the ground, Maria began to quietly dial the police downstairs. Her voice faintly echoed upstairs while Archibald seemed unaware of his aged hearing. Sawyer began to plead for the fight to stop, begging for a truce as his face radiated fear and defencelessness. His eyes knew by their look of despair that his employment was over but that his life was more important than his position.

"Mr Perkins! Please!" Sawyer cried.

Arch jumped up from his position on the floor as he took the stance of a linebacker preparing for a blitz. Sawyer's eyes widened in slow motion as he witnessed Archibald begin his charge. Sawyer was positioned in front of the railing after attempting to back out of the room to create distance, a scene I saw play out before anyone could do anything to stop it. Arch's shoulder dipped as Sawyer attempted to clear his path, but he was unsuccessful. As Arch met Sawyer, he used his large body to push him against the railing, holding him up while Sawyer's life flashed before his eyes.

"SAWYER!" I screamed in an attempt to make Arch reflect on what he was doing.

Archibald's eyes entered the shark-like state that Alè had reported earlier. I was unable to reach them in time as Arch used his full strength to throw Sawyer, who was half of his body weight, over the rail to the floor below.

As Sawyer's body began to free fall, my jaw unhinged as my pupils widened. Sawyer fell head first, landing directly on his neck. The sound produced was like biting down on raw pasta, making a vulgar crack that rippled across the whole palace. I looked at Archibald, but his face showed not a sliver of remorse. He looked slightly happy like he had accomplished something important.

Terrified, I let Arch waddle downstairs before getting up. As I walked over to the railing, I saw Sawyer's lifeless corpse laying with a neck angled the opposite way. He died on impact. No amount of EMS revival could bring him back. I practically vomited at the sight, a sight that barely made Archibald flinch. My knees gave out as I collapsed in front of the railing, practically fainting once again.

As I laid on the floor, I called emergency services and whispered the palace address as I cut off the operator's questions. I repeated about seven times that a killer was inside. I never wanted to involve the police. Maria already had. The police were my only chance of not leaving the palace in a polythene bag.

As I glanced over the railing, Maria screamed as she hovered over the corpse. Her wail would make anyone shudder from the sound alone. I heard Arch scold her from the front den like he was pleading for her silence.

"Wha-Wha-What did you do?" Maria stammered.

"He fell!"

"No, it can't be—"

"He fell! Theodore saw it too!" Arch said to Maria.

Maria began to frantically pace as I reached the bottom step. Seeing Sawyer's lifeless body up close made me dizzy.

"The hell he did!" I screamed as I walked into the foyer where Sawyer's body was.

"Sorry?" Arch yelled.

"He didn't fall!" I asserted.

"You must be confused. Sawyer attacked me while I simply defended myself. He tried to throw me over the railing before he slipped and fell himself!" Arch said, making each line up as he went.

"That doesn't even make sense! First of all—" I began to explain as I was cut off by Archibald's demand.

"Maria, Theodore, front den, now!"

"No!" I shouted.

Maria walked ahead of me, violently shaking in fear. She reluctantly shuffled her way into the den, sitting down on the sofa.

I entered the den as Archibald was now alone in there with her. I felt like I had to protect her, seeing how Arch was capable of cold-blooded murder. I knew the police would arrive within the next few minutes, so I just had to keep the two of us alive until then. My main goal was to stick beside Maria until their arrival.

"Sit! Both of you!

I grabbed a seat, holding Maria's hand to comfort her violent trembling.

"Now listen here. We will be calling an ambulance. The official story is that Sawyer had been helping Maria dust the chandelier, and he overextended his reach from the top railing. Sawyer, unfortunately, fell, causing his death. Nobody except for the three of us is to know of the altercation. That never happened. If you wish to protect yourselves, we all collaborate on this story when the medics get here."

Maria and I looked at each other in pure disgust.

"Do not include me in your lies, Archibald—"

"The only ticket you have out is my version," Arch interrupted me in a stern, collected tone.

"I will not lie!" Maria said with a fierce tone.

"Surely you know what happens. I go to jail for this. You two will not be around long enough to see my trial happen!"

"So you admit it! You did kill my mother!"

"No."

"Admit it!"

"It wasn't me," Archibald said as he cracked a slight grin.

"Liar!" I screamed.

"Well, I ordered the cheeseburger, but I didn't consume a single calorie," Archibald cackled in a demonic chant.

Enraged, I jumped up and socked Arch across the face. As my hand pulled back, his upper lip twitched, the iconic sign of his internal rage brewing.

"Hit me again faggot! This time, hit like a man!"

I backed down, not responding to his demands.

"Hit me again!" Archibald screamed.

"No!"

"Please, can all of this stop!" Maria cried while squeezing my hand.

Archibald jumped on top of me, pushing Maria to the floor. I kicked him in the groin, making his obese body roll off of the couch onto the hardwood floors in a violent thud. Maria sprinted out of the den while Arch was temporarily decommissioned.

As Archibald stood up, his eyes became shark-like once again. I was in the direct path of his stare, my life now in immense danger. The moment he charged me, I hopped over the couch like a gymnast, attempting to buy time by positioning myself with large furniture items between him and I. Arch shuffled around the couch as I hopped over the end table. The end table was tossed out of his way like it was made of cardboard. The table was solid oak but no match for the rage of Archibald Perkins. As I attempted to run, his fat arm snagged the back of my shirt, pulling me down to the ground in a swift, violent tug. My body collapsed, my bones producing a violent clanking sound as they collided with the floor.

Archibald stood over my body, still with shark-like eyes.

"I gave you an out. Why did it come to this?" Arch screamed.

I looked at Arch. His eyes no longer looked human. His mask was completely down, and his true demonic form stared back at me.

As Arch wrestled my body that was already on the ground, his arm closed around my neck.

"One last chance, tell me I'm innocent. Make me believe it, dammit!"

"Fuck off!" I gasped as his grip tightened.

"Let him go!" Maria screeched as she held up Archibald's missing hunting rifle.

Arch turned his attention to her and began to laugh hysterically.

"Doubt it's loaded," he said while disregarding her.

"LET. MY. SON. GO!"

"HA! Your son?" Arch repeated. "That's about the funniest thing I have ever heard. You will never be one of us. The Perkins stem from noble bloodlines! You are nothing but a poor Mexican maid with not a single drop of importance running through you," Arch cackled as he taunted Maria.

"Puerto Rican!" Maria shouted as she fired a round into the ceiling of the den.

The sound made the whole house shudder, causing Archibald's eyes to widen in pure shock.

"HA! You would never shoot me!"

Maria pointed the rifle directly at Archibald's chest, staring him directly in his dark soul as he tightened his grip on my throat. The air was becoming denser by the second, making my breathing burn like a hot ember that sat in my throat each time I inhaled.

The pounding on the front door echoed through the whole palace as three pairs of boots stormed the hardwood floors. As soon as Arch knew we had company, his grip loosened as he acted like a helpless victim, embracing my shoulders.

"Drop the gun now!"

Maria smiled at Archibald while he smirked back, believing there was no way out of this for her. His face was like that of an athlete who was about to win the whole tournament, soaked in victory.

"You took my second son, but not my third!" Maria smiled.

"DROP THE RIFLE NOW!" the officers shouted together.

BANG!

BANG! BANG! BANG!

Both Maria and the officers' guns fired almost simultaneously as she never broke her smile. A rifle bullet entered Archibald's chest, tearing chunks of flesh with it on the way out. As it exited, the life drained from his soulless eyes. His body collapsed beside mine, covering me in a pool of his royal blood.

As Maria fell, her smile never broke. The three bullets that pierced her lungs instantly caused them to collapse while her smile stayed put. As she laid on the floor, the rifle laid beside her in a pile of both her and Archibald's blood. She looked over to me, still smiling as her eyes shut for the last time. I reached out and screamed for her, but she was already gone. Archibald and Maria bled together. Their blood mixed into one uniform solution.

As I laid on the floor, the room became blurry while the apparitions of three officers circled around me. Their mouths were moving, but there was no sound.

Just like Maria and Archibald, my eyes became heavy as my soul entered into the void.

CHAPTER SIXTEEN

The bright blue-white lights practically injured my eyes as they opened. Confused, I turned my head to see a paramedic crouched beside me as she mouthed words that were completely unintelligible.

The words began to mumble into slight sentences, still unclear, like I had been speaking to a non-Anglophone who had been blurting out the limited vocabulary they knew.

As I turned my head to the other side, I quickly realized I was inside an ambulance. The medic's voice became partially clear as I heard her ramble on.

"Whrns-have-olfanfasd—your head?"

I stared her down, focusing on her mouth before the words began to become clear.

"Are you aware if you have hit your head?"

I shook my head to indicate I hadn't.

"Do you know your name?"

"Th-Theo!" I screeched in frustration as the words struggled to leave my mouth.

"Good!" she yelled enthusiastically. "And do you know your last?"

"P-Per-Perk—"

"Perk?" she repeated whilst trying to keep me talking.

I shook my head again.

"Du-Dubois."

"Dubois? Lovely name," the medic said with a smile. "Are you Québécois?"

"N-no, I'm the real type of French." I smiled.

"Hurtful! I'm half Québécois!" She grinned back, appearing happy that she got me to engage.

"Tabarnak! I'm sorry if I offended you!"

"None taken!" she laughed.

I was admitted to the hospital as the doctors wanted to assess me. I was physically intact but emotionally numbed. The image of a lifeless Maria made me convulse in shock. Her smile gutted me, like she considered herself to be a martyr.

I felt my pocket. The ring and my phone were the only contents inside. Pushing past the ring, I pulled my phone out, informing Wes where I was, letting him know I was alright. A few officers waited outside of my room, pleading with the doctors for permission to question me.

The first officer walked in, a notepad in one hand and a coffee in her other as she half-smiled at me.

"Theodore?" she said.

"Theo."

"Sorry, Theo, how are you feeling?" she asked with a soft mother-like stare.

"Like shit!" I smiled.

"I'm Detective Cindy Stimers."

"Wow! A lot of trouble you have been through in the past few days!" Detective Johan announced as he stepped into the room.

"Yup," I sarcastically added.

"Theo, if you don't mind, we would like to ask you some questions," Detective Stimers said.

"I guess."

Detective Johan gave me a stern glare before sitting down on the hospital armchair in my room.

"Firstly, If you could tell us how this all started, the incident."

"Dunno. I'm really confused—like, I'm trying to process it all."

"Well, let's start with the man found deceased upon the responding officer's arrival. They stated he appeared to have fallen, possibly having broken his neck."

I stared out the window past Johan and Stimers. My eyes zoned out, blocking them out temporarily. I knew if I told the truth, I would condemn myself once again.

"He fell."

"Fell?" Stimers repeated whilst taking rapid notes. "How did he fall?"

"Cleaning. He was cleaning the chandelier that hung over the foyer. He overextended his reach and fell."

Lying felt like I had swallowed a dagger, cutting my insides as I spewed the falsity.

"Do you know his name?"

"Sawyer, he worked for us."

"A cleaner, I suppose?" Johan asked.

"Yes. A chef who helped clean when he was not busy in the kitchen," I said.

Both detectives made notes with faces that appeared to believe my story. They genuinely seemed to agree that Sawyer's death was an accident. Either that or they were good at preventing their true thoughts from displaying across their faces.

"Okay now, let's move onto the scene that was reported when the officers arrived." Stimers said as she sipped on her coffee."You're the one who called the police the second time, but the first?"

"Maria," I said.

"And who is Maria?" Stimers asked.

Hearing her name made me cry uncontrollably. Both detectives rushed to my bed to comfort me, apologizing for overstepping.

"She-she—was like a mother to me," I said.

Both stopped asking questions, hoping I would spew groundbreaking information.

"Maria called the police. She was afraid for my life."

"Why would you think she felt that way?" Johan asked.

"Archibald was using slurs and trying to fight me."

"Mr Archibald Perkins, your father, correct?"

"Yes."

The room became silent. The only sound that carried across was the sound of their ballpoint pens on their lined paper.

"Arch got into a fight with me. I had told him something he didn't agree with. Archibald was a conservative man. Ask anyone and they will agree. Arch believed in the nuclear family and would do anything to defend it."

"What did you tell him that set him off?" Stimers asked.

"That I'm in love with a guy, my boyfriend, Wesley Summers."

"Oh, wow!" Stimers said with raised eyebrows.

"I told him I was in love about four times, and he told me he'd rather have a dead son than a gay son. He began to choke me out, and Maria saw what was happening. She begged him to stop ten times, but he wouldn't listen.

The air became denser as his grip tightened. He only let go when your officers arrived. Maria then shot him dead in my defence."

"So Maria murdered your father?" Stimers asked.

"No!" I yelled. "Maria saved my life! Maria is a hero!"

"She murdered your father, though." Johan asserted.

"No!" I repeated. "My father was acting crazy! He would have killed me!"

"So, your father had a vendetta out on the family members, then?" Johan said.

"GOD NO! He was not a serial killer, a simple man, really. He would have only killed me in a temporary fit of insanity, not because he planned it."

That was the hardest lie I told. I kept my eyes on the prize of survival

"So, she was acting in your defence then?" Stimers asked.

"She was defending me. Maria is a hero!" I shouted.

"She had time to not fire, as she was given a chance by all three officers to do so," Stimers added.

"NO!"

"Are you aware of any other—" Johan started as I cut him off in tears.

"What don't you cops understand? He would have killed me for being gay!" I screamed.

"I see," Johan said in a passive tone.

"And Sawyer falling was a completely separate issue?" Stimers asked with a curious stare.

"They had nothing to do with each other!"

"So they just happened at the same time?" Johan asked.

"Sawyer fell as the three of us were downstairs."

"The operator reported a young male, which we now know was you, talked about a killer being inside. Care to clarify?" Johan asked.

"Yes. I made the call from the back porch as I was scared for my life. Archibald threatened me, and I knew he was serious. He found a few texts from my boyfriend, then told me he was going to kill me. I panicked, and that's when I called the police. Archibald saw me on the phone outside, thinking I was calling my boyfriend, which made his homophobic rage intensify. I told him that I loved Wesley and that was when he began to choke me out. He was in a fit of rage!"

"I see." Stimers nodded.

I felt terrible for lying. The action made me disgusted with myself, but I needed to save my own life. This was my lifeboat on the sinking ship of the Perkins dynasty. Maria, Archibald, Sawyer, Sophie, and Alè were all dead. Nothing could change that. If the police saw Archibald as a temporarily insane homophobe who began choking his son in a moment of tension, the story could end there, case closed.

If I opened Pandora's box that Archibald was a deranged serial killer who would use his allies to wipe anyone out in his path, the police would have dug so deep that my grave would also be dug. I was alive and lucky to be. It gutted me knowing that Sawyer's family would never get the truth, but the truth condemned me. My version of the story made Domenico and his goons take pity on me. Domenico knew my father was insane. I knew Domenico was not going to be fazed by the fact Arch tried to kill his gay son in a fight over his sexuality.

Dom already knew he would kill his family members when enraged. I posed no threat to their empire by being the victim. I posed a threat by telling the truth. Domenico had no idea I knew the truth.

I didn't care if the detectives didn't believe me. They seemed unresolved as they exited my hospital room, but it didn't matter. I was the sole survivor, the sole witness. Whatever I said was the official story, as it coincided with their limited evidence and knowledge.

*

Wes pushed past the nurses standing in the hallway outside my room, forcing his way to my bed.

"T! What the hell!"

"I-I-I'm sor—"

"I was so scared!" Wes cried.

"I'm sorry!"

"Theodore, is this man with you?" my nurse called as she trailed behind Wes.

"Yes, this is my boyfriend!" I shouted.

The nurse exited, allowing Wes and me some privacy.

"I'm sorry, that was dumb."

"What happened?"

"I will explain. Arch, Maria, and Sawyer are dead!"

"Holy fuck!" Wes screamed.

"I love you," I whimpered as my eyes filled with tears.

"I love you too," he repeated as he jumped on my bed.

Wes and I laid in silence for two minutes as we both cried. I think the sight of me being so distraught made him cry harder. He stroked my hair to comfort me before I finally broke the silence.

"Maria shot Arch right in the chest," I whispered in his ear.

Wes' eyes widened as the information sunk in.

"Sawyer broke his neck. I'm the only one who survived."

"Jesus!"

"I'm sorry I only left you a note. I didn't want you to come after me."

"I would have been there for you. I love you, T!"

"That's why I couldn't tell you. I had to protect you from Arch!"

Wes held me, trying to grasp the reason for my secrecy.

"If you came with me, I couldn't have protected you, Wessy," I cried. "Look! Here we are, both safe in each other's arms."

Wes grabbed my neck, kissing me to relieve the tension. As we passionately interlocked lips, the nurse came in with a stack of forms she needed to discuss. We both ignored her for a two-second period, then I turned my attention to her.

"Theodore, I do need you to fill out some forms if you are able to," the nurse announced while smiling.

"Yeah, sure, I'll take them."

The first box asked me to fill in my surname. I froze for a second, not knowing what to write in its place.

Perkins seemed wrong, like it no longer fit. The dynasty was hanging by a thread. I had to sever it completely.

After twenty seconds of stillness, I signed the document as **Theodore Alexander Dubois**.

"I like it," Wes said.

"It ends here. All of it."

I laid with Wes for ten minutes as Jade rushed through the door, carrying a large bouquet of pink roses and a teddy bear from the gift shop in the main lobby.

"Had to show me up, huh, Jade?" Wes giggled.

"Besties before boyfriends!" Jade shot back with a smile before turning to me. "What the hell happened?"

I filled Jade in on the situation, making her sob when she found out Sawyer and Maria were dead. My father's death was merely skimmed over in comparison to theirs. Maria's death, in particular, gutted Jade. She knew Maria was like a mother to me, that I was now an orphan.

"I'm changing my last name to Dubois."

"Holy shit! I love that!" Jade cried.

"Well, for now, one day I'll save up some money for your sapphire and make it Summers," Wes gushed.

"Hmm. You're assuming I would say yes."

"I can be your best man!" Jade said.

"In Alè's place, you can be my best man, Jade," I said.

The three of us had a group cry, followed by a group hug. Jade and Wes were all I had left in the secular world. Despite all of the losses I endured, I knew how fortunate I was.

Wes refused to leave the whole time I was in the hospital. He sat in the uncomfortable armchair in my room, grabbing me coffee and meals so I didn't have to eat the rank hospital food.

Seeing that I was physically unharmed, the hospital released me the next morning. Wes had ordered a ride on his app to get to the hospital, so we had to order one back to his apartment.

"I'm not letting you pay for the ride home!"

"Home?"

"Yeah. The apartment is now home. If you want it to be, of course," Wes replied.

"I do." I smiled. "I'm paying, Wessy."

"Good luck."

"Trust me, I can afford it now," I said with a grin.

"Wait, holy fuck!" Wes screamed. "Is Prince T now —K-King T?"

"King T indeed," I said. "I wear the crown now."

"And as King, what is your first act?"

"To abolish the monarchy."

*

A week later, the police finally released the details of the incident to the press. I awoke to a few summaries of my lies, a sickening yet liberating feeling.

ARCHIBALD PERKINS FOUND GUNNED DOWN IN-SIDE HIS MILTON MANSION

Police responded to a 911 call at the Perkins residence. Archibald Perkins, 52, was alive when officers arrived on the scene. Maria Hermosa Fernandez, a staff member of Perkins, shot him with a hunting rifle after ignoring the responding officers' demand to stand down. Perkins died shortly after Fernandez fired. Police responded to Fernandez's gunfire with their own. Fernandez died shortly after due to gunshot wounds from the officers.

Perkins leaves behind one living son, Theodore Perkins, aged 18, reportedly home at the time of Archibald's death.

Upon their arrival, a deceased unnamed man was found, which is reported by Halton Police as a non-suspicious incident unrelated to the murder of Perkins. The family of the deceased has requested his identity to remain undisclosed.

ARCHIBALD PERKINS SHOT! BLED OUT IN FRONT OF SON

Local socialite Archibald Perkins was reportedly shot in front of his son, Theodore Perkins, by their maid, Maria. The internet has nicknamed her the "Maria the Murder-ous Maid of Milton."

Theodore Perkins is now set to inherit the family's vast fortune at the young age of eighteen. We have reached out to the family but have yet to receive a response. More details to follow.

ARCHIBALD PERKINS MURDERED BY HIS MAID

A fight reportedly broke out over financial issues in the Perkins' home. Our sources reported longtime maid, Maria Fernandez, was severely underpaid for years.

Fernandez shot Perkins after he denied giving her a raise. Our sources cannot confirm whether or not the non-suspicious reported death was also due to Maria's rage. We speculate Fernandez may have had something to do with the death, but this is not confirmed.

Maria, having been painted as an unhinged murderer, lit a flame of rage in my soul. She was anything but. She lost her dignity so that I could keep my life, her ultimate sacrifice for me. I was forever indebted to Maria, a debt I could never repay.

CHAPTER SEVENTEEN

Five years had passed, and I, Theo Dubois, had killed Theodore Jacob Henry Perkins I. The rate at which things had changed in just five years was indescribable. After being released from the hospital, I kept true to my word and filed for a legal name change.

Wes and I lived together in secrecy for six months in his apartment before we broke the news to his parents. Wes' parents immediately accepted me as one of their own the moment we shared the news of us living together. It was like the knowledge that we lived together solidified with them that I was serious about my and their son's relationship. They knew we were boyfriends, but the shock of us practically living like a married couple was too much to dump at once, hence why we waited to break it to them. Mr and Mrs Summers always wanted me to refer to them as John and Helen, but referring to them by their first names felt unnatural to me. Some of the habits I picked up in my upbringing didn't die.

Upon the death of Archibald, I became the sole survivor and heir to the Perkins family fortune. At just the age of eighteen, I had more wealth than most people would ever accumulate in their lifetime. Every asset, including Perkins Palace, Archibald's cars, and the personal investments of each of my family members, was now mine. Altogether, my portfolio of inherited wealth sat around two-hundred million dollars, a sum passed onto me the moment that Maria fired Arch's rifle.

Perkins Palace was in my possession after the investigation concluded. Unable to find significant evidence to dispute my story, the investigation came to an abrupt end. I suspected both Detective Johan and Stimers didn't buy my story, but there was nothing they could do as I was the sole witness.

After I took the palace, I cleared out my things with Wes, trembling the entire time just being inside that sinister building. The whole time we loaded boxes, the ring clinked around in my pocket, practically slipping out at times. I considered leaving it at the palace, but I wanted to ensure it was going to disappear forever, not enter into circulation once again at some pawn shop. I sold all of Archibald's personal items, including his jewellery, furniture, and other prized possessions, except for the orange beauty. She was mine.

The estate sale lasted two weeks, the palace being stripped further with each day that passed. After auctioning all the palace belongings, the value of the paintings, jewellery, and antiques equated to ten million dollars. I gave Maria's family and Sawyer's family all of their personal belongings, along with five million dollars each in their own respective trust funds. No amount of money would have restored their families, but I hoped the money could alleviate some of the burden.

Once the palace was emptied, I left it to decay like the rest of the Perkins. Eventually, I signed the land away to developers. I could not bring another generation of pernicious Perkins to plague the property. The land needed to heal, as did I. I signed the contract with one condition. When the developers built their proposed subdivision, they had to name one of the streets Sawyer Boulevard, and one Maria Lane.

As agreed upon, both streets were included in the site plans when construction began a few years later. The property was used to build a subdivision large enough for three hundred homes. Three hundred families of the working class, my final act of spite to the noble Lord Archibald, the working class using his former land.

One night after the construction crews had left, I parked the orange beauty on an old side road, a ten-minute walk off-site. Following the old creek that Alè and I played in as kids, I crept onto the vacant job site undetected in the dark of night. With a trowel in my right hand and the maple signet ring in my left, I dug a small hole on the gravel road of Maria Lane before the pavement was laid. I placed the ring in the gravel, then packed it down with my foot. I left before anyone could see me.

A few days later, the signet ring was solidified into the earth by a ten-tonne compactor. Maria once again protected me.

Domenico lost his main connection within Ontario, causing his crown to slip from his head as soon as the rifle fired. In his place, I assumed other criminals amalgamated the territory into their own. The ring was meant to fall from his hand. He was no longer the king he considered himself to be. I contemplated going back to the police, knowing that Dom had lost his powerful grip, but this also condemned me to a possible criminal record. I lied to multiple detectives to save myself, not something I could easily back out of, so I knew I had to stick to the story I had told since day one. I knew Domenico had bad things coming for him, though. You can only be so slop-py for so long before it comes back to haunt you. Sloppy kings always fall, always.

Domenico never once acknowledged Archibald's death. Not a single white rose, not even a simple note of condolence, came from him. To be fair, I never held a funeral for Archibald. His remains were cremated, but I never picked them up. His entire existence was limited to a brown cardboard box on a shelf with his name on a white label. Eventually, the funeral home stopped trying to contact me. I assumed they did what funeral homes did for unclaimed remains, a mass gravesite. Archibald laying with commoners instead of having a large marble monument made me feel fulfilled. He was lucky I al-lowed him to be cremated. He deserved to sink in the depths of dirty, smelly Lake Ontario in concrete shoes.

Maria and Sawyer were each given a marble monu-ment on my father's plot. With their families' permis-sion, I buried both of them side-by-side in Archibald's massive pre-purchased gravesite. I had to use it for something. I also donated five-million dollars to the pri-vate cemetery in Maria's name. In response to my large donation, the cemetery built a small park inside the gates called 'Mariposita Park.' Two large oak wood benches faced each other within a circle of beautiful bushes of lavender and rounded boxwoods. They also planted a small maple tree, a stark contrast to the decrepit one from Perkins Palace. One bench had an iron plaque with Sawyer's name, and one had Maria's. The peaceful little park, in all of its beauty, made anyone who sat there calm, whatever issue was on their minds, as the floral scent of lavender worked its magic. It was an ode to how Sawyer and Maria made me feel at peace.

Alè and my mother were buried in the same cemetery as Maria and Sawyer. I had the monumental mason replace Alè's headstone. It no longer read Perkins, but instead Dubois, the name I wanted to remember him by, his true chosen name. A few of the distant Perkins, third cousins and such, were all disgusted by my actions. I considered this a win, a further separation from the distant Perkins. I wanted my future children to never even meet a Perkins, and that made the chances a whole lot better.

My mother was buried as Sophie Dubois, the woman she truly was. She never was a Perkins. She only played one like an actor on a stage. Arch never considered her one, so it was fitting to not give her that dishonourable title in death. Sophie Perkins was a socialite. Sophie Dubois was a mother, a friend, a lover, and a soul free from the shackles of the Perkins curse.

*

Wes and I outgrew the studio apartment after two years of living together. Our things were practically swallowing us whole, like two hoarders living in a hotel room. I used my inheritance to purchase a penthouse downtown, a luxury building with state-of-the-art modern finishes. The lobby smelled of pine and white tea as soon as you walked through the massive glass doors off of the street. Our unit had two floors, a bit much for two people, but we planned to expand our two-person family one day. Wes and I decorated the great room to our taste with a large black grand piano, brown leather sofas, and a large abstract painting of bright, beautiful butterflies.

Our kitchen was a true chef's kitchen. In Sawyer's honour, I learned how to properly cook in it. I spent hours studying the culinary arts, recreating his iconic dishes. Every time I tasted something I cooked that tasted remotely like his, a tear would come to my eye. I knew he was proud of me like his spirit lived on through me when I was in the kitchen.

I also added a large espresso machine in the kitchen, one of the fancy machines from Italy. Each morning, I woke up early to bring Wes a flat white in bed. He never expected it from me, but I just did it. Wes deserved it. He was my rock when my family crumbled. He deserved so much more than just a coffee in bed every morning.

*

One night after a fancy dinner, Wes insisted on going for a stroll through the downtown core. We walked along Front Street for what seemed like twenty minutes, something that I was not prepared for in my stiff leather oxfords. The concrete colliding with the soles of my dress shoes made my feet ache.

"Wes! Where are we going?"

"I'll tell you when we get there!"

"Wow, that's helpful!" I grinned.

"It's a secret!" Wes said.

I followed Wes into Union Station, a place we only ever visited if we left the city. He led me through The Great Hall without saying a single word.

"Where are we going?"

"Nowhere."

Confused, I began contemplating all of the reasons Wes would bring me to Union. I knew he liked the food court downstairs, but I knew we just ate a twelve-course tasting menu that filled both of us by course six.

As I looked up at the ceilings, something I did every time I walked through The Great Hall, I turned around to see Wes on one knee.

"The-The-Theodore Alexander Dubois—"

"Wha-What are you do-doing?" I cut in.

"Theodore Alexander Dubois," Wes stammered. "Will you be a Summers?"

Wes began to cry while he looked up at me. The whole action caught me off guard, my face radiating shock as the crowd of onlookers circled around us.

"I do," I whispered as tears filled my eye.

Wes, while crying, slid a massive blue sapphire ring on my ring finger. The sapphire was enormous, appearing to be at least five carats. The sapphire with its diamond halo was as wide as my finger.

"How many flat whites did this cost?" I laughed.

"It's a secret," Wes said as he leaned in to kiss me.

The crowd all cheered as we passionately interlocked lips inside the station. A few people even congratulated us as if they were old friends.

I walked out of Union, the place where Wes and I met only five years ago, only this time with my fiancé by my side. Wes kept looking back at me, his eyes sparkling the same colour as my ring. In Wes' eyes, I now knew what family meant.

On the thirty-first of August the next year, I married Wesley Summers at noon in front of the whole Summers family with the Alberta mountains in the background. We selected a beautiful outdoor venue near Banff.

At the ceremony, we left four seats empty in the first row. Each seat had a small reserved card, one for Alè, Maria, Sawyer, and my mother. If Archibald was alive, he wouldn't have shown up nor been invited in the first place. In Alè's place, Jade was my best man. She even wore a tuxedo as she took her role seriously. My gift to her was a solid-gold cardinal brooch, something she wore with pride on her tuxedo lapel after learning the significance.

Lisanne walked me down the aisle, smiling from ear to ear as she gave me away. I stumbled a few times saying my vows, which made Wes's eyes sparkle as his smile grew each time. He loved me for who I was, for better, for worse, in sickness and in health.

Our venue was a grassy field with a dramatic view of the Alps. A series of white tents were laid across the lawn with string lights connecting each when night fell. Wes' parents both made speeches that made me tear up multiple times. We both loved him just as much. He was our incredible man. Each table had bouquets of white peonies, my selection. I didn't invite a single distant Perkins. I knew they had the means to travel, but they were not welcome in my new life. Part of me felt incredibly guilty, but part of me felt I had made the right decision. I had the only family that mattered here with me. I was now a Summers anyways.

*

After our honeymoon in Turks and Caicos, I spent a week in the guest room of our penthouse going through old photos of Alè, the only photos I kept when Perkins Palace was wiped clean. It took a while to locate the only photo where Alè looked genuinely happy. Even if he was smiling, his eyes still looked disheartened by the weight of his problems in the others. I wished I could have done more to help him, but I knew I had to stop blaming myself.

The photos of his gloomy face were too hard to look at, ripping at my heartstrings each time I flipped the pages of the albums. I sorted each of the photos into two piles, ones where he looked depressed and ones where he seemed genuinely happy. The depressed pile was nearly two-hundred photos high. In contrast, the happy pile consisted of one singular photo.

The only happy photo had been taken by Maria on Alè's eighth birthday. Archibald and my mother had been on vacation in Bora Bora, so Maria took it upon herself to throw Alè a party in their absence. Alè was allowed to invite all of his friends, even the ones Archibald despised. Surrounded by his closest friends without a single sneer from Archibald, Alè was genuinely happy, something that only lasted until Arch's plane touched down in Toronto.

The next morning, Wes had gone out with his friends for brunch. He invited me, but I had other plans. I grabbed the two piles, setting the happy photo into its own album, keeping it safe. I grabbed a stock pot from the kitchen and took the pile of disturbing photos out to the balcony. I reviewed each photo once again, tears streaming down my face as most of them had awful memories attached.

Some of the memories made me violently shake, sending chills down my spine that radiated across my whole body. They were not photos of Alè. They were photos of the person that Archibald created. Every taunting jab, every name, every physical altercation that took place in these photographs was no longer allowed to exist in my home, in my new life.

I ignited the first ten, and the negative energy crumbled into ash as they floated away in the wind of downtown Toronto. The rest of the photos followed suit, lifting more and more weight off of my shoulders with each photo that incinerated. Alè was not weak but rather a product of a strong spirit fighting evil every day. No matter how strong Alè was, daily physical and mental abuse from the person that gave him life, wore him down. I was never as strong as my brother. That was why I was still alive. I allowed all of it to happen, only countering Archibald in Alè's last year of life. By then, it was too late.

That year I grew strong but never acquired half of the strength of my brother. Alè had defied Archibald for nineteen years while I only did it for one. Despite what Archibald tried to assert, King Alexander the Affectionate held the title of 'The Stronger Brother.'

SCAN ME FOR MORE INFO!